A guilty sort of exhilaration

charged him up as he drove a little faster on the way home. He was barely in his driveway before he had the car parked and the vial in his hands. Twisting the cap off, he tapped some of the white powder onto a knuckle and breathed it in with a sharp inhale.

The rush went right to his head, like bubbles in soda soaring upwards, popping at the surface.

"Fuck yeah. Holy *shit*…" he moaned, body sagging back into his seat.

As key ties holding his mind together slowly became unraveled, he saw in his memory that contract. It was all there. His name, his information, his preferences and lack of boundaries — except one — were all there in black and white, undeniable. There was something pure about that, having it all written down, tucked in a manila folder and placed on the desk of a cocky, hard-bodied, big-dicked Dominant who hadn't hesitated in grabbing hold of Kyle's cock to see how he'd react. God, he couldn't wait. As formal and safe as it was to submit to a Dominant in a professional setting, as the result of a business arrangement between consenting adults, it was also unspeakably dangerous, especially for someone like Kyle.

If you enjoy this collection, you can sign up for a free membership at ForbiddenFiction.com and discuss it with other readers and the author at the *Threshold* story page at forbiddenfiction.com/library/collection/LK1-1.100007. We do our best to proof all our work, but if you spot a text error we missed, please let us know via our website Contact Form at forbiddenfiction.com/contact.

Also recommended...

You may also enjoy these other ForbiddenFiction works:

 **Entering the House of Silence by J.A. Jaken**
Four young men find themselves drawn to the service of the House of Silence, the famous brothel that caters to the whims of the elite and powerful. One of them discovers how intense that service can be. An anthology of stories set in the House of Silence. (M/M)
https://forbiddenfiction.com/library/collection/JAJ-1.100003

 **Don't... by Jack L. Pyke**
"Don't... open me." Three simple words that tease Jack, taking him places from his dark past. For Jack, BDSM is a way to resist his worst impulses. Yet, the stranger calling himself The Unknown seeks to use that to seduce him. As Jack slips further down into the abyss, two men hold the power to save him. Will it be Gray, the Master who knows Jack's every secret? Or Jan, the first man to give Jack a reason to hope? With deadly ghosts coming out to play, Jack may lose everything, even his life. (M/M)
http://forbiddenfiction.com/library/story/JP2-1.000134

Threshold

a Society of Masters anthology

by Lynn Kelling

ForbiddenFiction
www.forbiddenfiction.com

an imprint of

Fantastic Fiction Publishing
www.fantasticfictionpub.com

THRESHOLD
A Forbidden Fiction book

Fantastic Fiction Publishing
Hayward, California

© Lynn Kelling, 2014

CREDITS
Editors: D.M. Atkins, Rylan Hunter, Lon Sarver
Cover Design: Siolnatine
Cover art: Cheschhh at Dreamstime
Internal cover art: Newphotoservice at Dreamstime and Alexander Lyubavin at Pixmac; Studio-54-foto at Dreamstime; Honored at Dreamstime; Purmar at Dreamstime; Smilla at Dreamstime; Marco Zilli at Dreamstime; Benjamin Franklin Bridge photo By Ben Yanis [CC-BY-2.0, via Wikimedia Commons]. Model photo by Curaphotography at Dreamstime.
Internal cover design: D.M. Atkins and Siolnatine
Production Editor: Erika L Firanc
Proofreading: Morgan Kailin, Siolnatine

SKU: LK1-100007-01 FFP
ISBN: 978-1-62234-187-0

Published in the United States of America

DISCLAIMER

This book is a work of fiction which contains explicit erotic content; it is intended for mature readers. Do not read this if it's not legal for you.

All the characters, locations and events herein are fictional. While elements of existing locations or historical characters or events may be used fictitiously, any resemblance to actual people, places or events is coincidental.

This book depicts depicts fictional BDSM; it is not intended to be used as an instruction manual. It contains descriptions of erotic acts that may be immoral, illegal, or unsafe. The characters are not models for the Safe, Sane and Consensual forms embraced by most current practitioners of BDSM. The authors take license with the use of BDSM for dramatic effect. Do not take the events in this story as proof of the plausibility or safety of any particular practice.

Author's Foreward

Each of the stories in this anthology are part of ForbiddenFiction's Society of Masters, a shared world in which most of my characters live and interact in mostly subtle ways. Jack L. Pyke's *Don't...* series also exists in this shared world, and our characters cross over throughout multiple novels, including *Forgive Us (Deliver Us 3)* and *Breakdown*. In the following pages, you will find short stories featuring Travis Saxon and Avery Williams from *Whatever the Cost*, and Gabriel Hunter, Darrek Grealey, Ben Knox and Kyle Roth from *Deliver Us*.

One thing that is important to note is that all of the works within the Society of Masters exist on the same timeline. There is a precise order to everything that happens. The stories collected here either take place before the *Deliver Us* series and *Whatever the Cost*, or give insight into moments not covered by the novels.

Now, you might be wondering what these two groups of characters have to do with each other and how they are connected. Though Trace doesn't actually make an appearance in the stories within this book, he is the connection between *Deliver Us* and *Whatever the Cost*. It is revealed in *Forgive Us*, that Trace, Founder of the private BDSM club Diadem and patriarch of his circle of friends in *Deliver Us*, devoted a decade of his life to an organization known as The Company. The Company employs prostitutes under unbreakable contracts for ten years at a time. Just as Trace sacrificed much of his youth serving the whims of wealthy clientele in less than ideal circumstances, so do two men named Avery Williams and Travis Saxon, whose relationship is the subject of *Whatever the Cost*.

Trace, Avery, and Travis share more than just mutual friends and enemies. Their time with The Company shapes who they are. Three stories in this anthology — *Escape, Between Here and There*, and *Trick or Truth* — explore the lives Avery and Travis leave behind when they decide life as a prostitute is the more desirable option. Like Trace, they have strong motivation for signing away so many years, no matter what that span of time might bring.

I will say that those three stories contain some of the most intense moments out of everything I have written. With *Escape*, it was something I knew I had to write, for Travis's sake and in tribute to the man he becomes. Eventually, Travis leaves his name behind along with his family, and transforms into Jacen, just as Avery becomes Liam. The trials of Jacen's childhood were something not delved into in detail in *Whatever the Cost*, but they were a key motivator in the development of his identity. There is a very specific devil hiding in Jacen's closet, and Jacen likes to think it will stay locked up for good. But, his journey was never going to be complete until I gave him the chance to face those horrors with the man he loves at his side, lending strength. Forcing Jacen to *go there* one more time was honestly difficult for me to do, but I, along with Liam, only love him more for being able to do it.

Between Here and There and *Trick or Truth* work hand in hand. I wrote them in that order, a heart wrenching before and after that has haunted me ever since. Avery's innocence in *Between Here and There* still brings tears to my eyes. It is his shining moment, where he was just a sweet boy with his whole heart bursting with love. In *Trick or Truth*, he is a little farther down the path of his life, and holding on so hard, you can feel it tearing him apart. It's not an easy read, but I hope you find it worth the pain, because part of me will always be there, with Avery, begging him to hold on just a little longer and whispering promises that it will get better.

Expected Lies, *Divine Surrender*, and *Never Happened* take place in that order on the Society of Masters timeline. *Expected Lies* gives a rare glimpse into Darrek and Kyle's teenage years. It's prom night of their senior year in high school, but it's a far from typical evening for these two. There are so many lies woven around what's going on, some of them by Kyle, others by Darrek. The game of it all is a dangerous psychological balancing act. They each play at it, working so hard not to knock everything askew, entirely out of self-preservation. I truly enjoyed exploring this part of their lives, when these two boys were forced to adapt and fight to save each other while simultaneously laying traps they were bound to fall into sooner or later.

Divine Surrender is the tale of how Ben and Kyle met. If you have read the *Deliver Us* books, you know that Ben is not your typical Master, and Kyle is far from your typical slave. Kyle's past is the monster waiting to lunge from behind, ripping and tearing, and he knows it. But he is absolutely willing to do whatever it takes to keep Ben from knowing it. So, there is a poisonous thread that slips through this sweet story, and the characters dance around it gingerly. Otherwise, there is plenty of humor and heat in the beginnings of the complex relationship they embark upon. But, there are also answers to questions like why Kyle chooses Ben over everyone else, over and over again, and why, from the start, Ben knew he could never walk away from Kyle. It is one of my personal all-time favorite pieces, and I hope it helps you fall for these guys just as hard as I have.

Never Happened, the first to be written out of this batch, was inspired by the inappropriate but undeniable chemistry between Gabriel and Ben in *Deliver Us*, and in seeking to reveal what their relationship was like before Darrek came along to further complicate things. It's a steamy little guilty pleasure, but sometimes those are the best kind.

Pleasures of Paradise takes place after *Deliver Us* and before *From Temptation (Deliver Us 2)*, when Gabriel and Darrek celebrated their two year anniversary with a trip to a tropical island in the Florida Keys catering only to the Masters and slaves of the BDSM community. This story grew from an excerpt removed from *From Temptation* mainly because it was too lighthearted to jibe with the tone of the rest of the book. Only a hint of this trip remains in the novel, but here you'll get to spend more time with the guys as Gabriel savors the decadence of leisurely testing each one of his submissive's limits, giving Darrek just the right irresistible motivation to conquer his fears and take a chance.

I'm deeply appreciative to everyone who helped inspire and motivate me to write the seven stories that make up *Threshold*, which taught me more about these characters than I'd have ever thought possible. More than that, though, they gave me a deeper appreciation for the trials people suffer in silence every day, and they give me hope than even when there seems to be no way out, bravery, perseverance, and love will help us find a way.

Thank you so much for reading and welcome to the Society of Masters.

—Lynn Kelling

Contents

Expected Lies

As Darrek reluctantly prepares for prom night, Kyle watches on with amusement. Darrek is frustrated with Kyle's lack of interest in bringing a girl to the prom and staying by his side, but Kyle is unphased by his best friend's increasingly strange emotional responses. Kyle has plans of his own that involve far less fancy clothing—far less clothing at all, really. Little does he know the extent of Darrek's determination to get what he wants. (M/M)

Expected Lies

In relative silence, seventeen-year-old Darrek Grealey gets dressed in a rented tuxedo, checking each item in the mirror's reflection as he puts it on to make sure he doesn't have it upside down or backwards. He might not have a lot of experience with formal wear, but it fits him like he does, highlighting his impressive height and build. His light brown, sun streaked hair has always been longer than his parents liked. It hangs loose about his shoulders. His brown, almond-shaped eyes reflect an innate sweetness he doesn't necessarily feel. The picture he makes becomes slowly more complete—one of a young man trying to be comfortable appearing to be more than he feels he is, more mature, more fully formed, more confident. As he is transformed, in appearance at least, into a gentleman, he is transported farther and farther from the meager confines of his childhood bedroom. An era of his life is ending, a new one beginning, and, in some ways, he has already fled to explore what waits.

Abandoned in Darrek's wake, sitting cross-legged and slouching on the bed behind him, Kyle Roth seems very much the lesser of the two. He is shorter, slimmer, and cute rather than manly. He's not mature, and doesn't pretend to be. In jeans and a worn-thin, grey t-shirt, he's not nearly as impressive-looking as Darrek in his tux. It's his posture too, though. The way he curls in on himself makes him appear even smaller than he is, more vulnerable and younger. As Darrek slips on his jacket and fits a cuff link in his shirt sleeve, Kyle watches on from what seems a great distance. Their prospects set the two adolescent men apart. They might as well be in separate worlds.

Darrek catches the sadness hiding in Kyle's glances. Kyle might be pretending to be above it all, but just the fact that he's there, watching Darrek get ready, tells Darrek all he needs to know.

"Need a hand?" Kyle offers when Darrek has trouble with the cuff link.

"Nah, I'm good. You could still come with, you know. You should. We'd have a great time."

"Come to prom?" The incredulous scorn in his tone is a stark contrast to the reality of his presence in Darrek's room, lending moral support as Mr. and Mrs. Grealey wait downstairs to take photos of Darrek and his date before the attractive couple is chauffeured to the big event.

"Yeah," Darrek says with encouragement. "It's not too late. You've got some nice suits at home."

The hopeful beseeching flips the switch on Kyle's resentment. "Why? Give me one good reason. Goofy monkey suits, awful music, social horrors. Lame."

Finally getting the cuff link in place, Darrek pushes his overlong hair back behind an ear and starts to fix the other sleeve, wearily raising an eyebrow at his best friend. Kyle, with his wide, bright blue eyes and God-given good looks, is restlessly combing his fingers through his light blond hair, grown long enough in front to almost cover his eyes but cut short in the back; shrinking in on himself, growing paler the longer he's planted on Darrek's bed, like the bed itself is toxic to his well-being.

"I'm sure one of your girlfriends was hoping you'd ask her to go. You could've gotten lucky," Darrek adds, playing to Kyle's inner horn dog. "We'd have had a great time. I mean, come on. It's the last big party before graduation."

"Not my kind of party. And who says I'm not getting lucky?"

"But you've been talking about moving away, right?" Darrek continues, not giving up. "You might never see a lot of these people again. Don't you care about that?"

Kyle scrunches his nose with dismissive boredom. He's been quieter than normal all day and it has gotten on Darrek's nerves. Whenever Kyle withdraws into his head like this it sets Darrek off, leaving him increasingly more agitated by the moment, unable to calm down until he figures out what's wrong. Taking care of Kyle has always been at the forefront of Darrek's priorities ever since they were little kids. With such absentee parents, no siblings or other close friends, Darrek is the entirety of Kyle's support system. It's a big job for someone so young and who is still figuring things out for himself, too.

"Okay, hotshot," Darrek counters. "I'll bite. Who are you getting lucky with?"

Kyle almost smiles at this. It plays at the edges of his lips and Darrek is captivated by the subtle twist, his sleeves forgotten. Shaking shaggy golden hair from his eyes, even in his grungy clothes, Kyle looks good. Darrek can't seem to look away. All of the years they've been close friends, the nights and days they've spent in this very room together—it stretches out behind them like a road and all that's in front of them now is a door. Darrek doesn't know what's waiting on the other side, but he suspects Kyle might have a clue. Do their paths go off in opposite directions or continue on together? It breaks Darrek's heart to wonder, so he stops himself from trying.

"Sophomore," Kyle tells him, smiling only with those twinkling blue eyes. "So fuckin' tight, you wouldn't believe it... makes me come so hard..."

"Jesus, Kyle." Darrek shakes his head, unable not to chuckle a little at Kyle's brazen façade. "Smells like bullshit to me. What's her name?"

Without missing a beat, Kyle answers, "Nicky."

"Nicky who?"

Kyle shrugs, unable to be bothered with details like surnames.

"I don't believe you for a second. I think you're gonna head home to that big empty house, get trashed on Daddy's booze and get lucky huggin' the porcelain in the bathroom while you barf up your 'good time'."

Ready to prove Darrek wrong, Kyle raises his eyebrows and pulls out his phone. It takes a second for him to remember the number and dial it. Putting the phone to his ear, he says after a moment, "Hey. Yeah, Nicky? It's Kyle. You around? Yeah? Let's meet at my place in an hour. Parents are gone. We'll use the pool. Yeah. Later."

"Damn," Darrek murmurs when Kyle has hung up. "Well. My bad, I guess."

"Apology accepted, ya big gorilla," Kyle smirks. "Have fun doing the Electric Slide with Sara."

Groaning with dread, Darrek turns away, putting his back to Kyle and checking his reflection as he smoothes his jacket. Kyle laughs.

Soon Darrek is standing out on the almost unnaturally green, weed-free lawn in front of carefully manicured shrubbery, his arm slung around Sara in her slinky, low-cut, sequined dress. Her laboriously styled hair smells of hairspray and too much fruity perfume. Darrek puts on as much of a smile as he can manage while feeling so uncomfortable as his mother relentlessly snaps photographs, his father looking on proudly. Kyle lurks a small distance away out by the road, biting his thumb to hide a wide smile brought of amusement at Darrek's predicament.

That's when Darrek knows he has made a mistake.

After all of his countless attempts to convince Kyle to go with him and the rest of their small circle of friends to the big, important dance, it hasn't hit Darrek until this very moment that maybe Kyle was right all along. Who cares if it's expected and tradition to go to prom? Kyle will be moving out of town soon, possibly out of state. Darrek should be sneaking beer and going swimming with his best friend while he still can, not wearing an incredibly constricting, heavy and ridiculous tuxedo, pretending to be excited about a long night of parading around the dolled-up girl on his arm and dancing badly in front of the whole school.

The photo session ends. Sara leaves Darrek to go and join the other girls who pour out of the rented limousine to gush over each other's dresses. The other tuxedo-clad guys grunt hellos to Darrek, looking as confused and awkward as he feels. Still lurking, Kyle doesn't try to hide his grin any more. He slides up to Darrek's side and whispers sarcastically, "Have a *great* time, Dare. Make sure you do your mama and daddy proud and treat her like a lady. You know where I'll be if you change your mind."

He winks at Darrek and holds his gaze for a long moment, like he's waiting to see if Darrek will get the joke, but not expecting him to. Something dark and slick moves between them, invisible but no less tangible, that Darrek can't get hold of; the truth is like an eel that slips through his fingers. But just brushing against it — those fleeting emotions — brings Darrek a taste of bitter shame, clawing terror, excruciating pain, damning lust and raw urgency.

Again, he gets the sense that Kyle sees this whole mess that is their lives so clearly, much more so than Darrek does himself, and Darrek wants that clarity too. He wants to grab hold of Kyle, wipe that knowing smirk from his lips and make him tell. Fuck the prom. Fuck Sara and the other guys and traditional milestones and all of that bullshit. This, right here with Kyle, is the only thing worth exploring. It's the only thing worth *anything*.

"Don't be late, now," Mr. Grealey says loudly from a few feet away, his gaze locked to his son.

At the sound of his father's commanding voice, everything that had just filled Darrek's head dissolves instantly away, forgotten.

"Yes, sir," Darrek says dutifully.

"Have a great time."

With a pit of dread and dissatisfaction causing a vague sickly feeling in his gut, Darrek answers, "Thanks. We will."

It's more like two hours rather than one before Nicky finally shows up. They meet around the side of the house. Kyle brings out two opened beers hooked in the fingers of one hand, with a handful of condoms palmed discreetly in the other. Unable to even attempt to disguise how happy he is to see Nicky—who is all tantalizing caramel skin, soft, dark hair and full, sensual lips—Kyle offers one of the drinks and chuckles as Nicky leans in to suck a firm, hungry kiss to his lips before even taking the beer.

"I wasn't sure if you were kidding about the pool," Nicky admits, indicating his swim trunks with a nod, twisting the shirt off of his head before grabbing the bottle from Kyle's hand. Upending it, Nicky drinks down a deep swallow, his throat working around the liquid, Adam's apple bobbing, before exhaling heavily with satisfaction.

They walk into the backyard. Kyle pauses to latch the tall wooden fence's gate. The sun is setting, but the in-ground pool is lit from within, casting ripples of entrancing blue light over the yard. An amber glow spills out from the back of the house as well. The night is pleasantly warm. All Kyle wears is a small, slim-fitting pair of trunks that ride low on his hips.

Kyle gestures to the patio furniture by the edge of the pool, drawing Nicky there, and tosses the condoms at one of the larger lounge chairs. He takes a long pull from the mouth of his beer and sets that down, too, before bringing Nicky close with a hand wrapping his slim waist. Kyle unties the drawstring of Nicky's swim shorts and pushes a hand greedily down inside them, grabbing a handful of him. He's ready for the next kiss as Nicky cups the back of Kyle's head and starts to plunder his mouth. It's rough, needy, and the eagerness in the tongue-fucking Kyle receives tells him that Nicky's probably hoping to top him this time, but it isn't going to happen. Kyle only bottoms for one person, and that person is not Nicky.

They break apart as Kyle pushes Nicky at the chair. "Lie down," he rasps, hard and ready, both of them aware that Kyle only called for one reason.

Nicky lowers himself onto the cushions and Kyle thinks fleetingly of how funny it was to get to somewhat honestly talk about his plans for the night with Darrek. The only lie had been that Nicky is a junior, not a sophomore, but since Darrek thinks Nicky is a *girl*, Kyle had thought there would be less of a chance of Darrek being familiar with the names of the sophomore girls in their school. Sick to death of hiding who he is and what he wants, Kyle is making a concerted effort to stop lying as much as has become commonplace for him, even if that means resorting to misdirection instead while he figures out how to come out of the closet he's stuck himself in for so long.

"Oh, we're going swimming," Kyle assures Nicky, climbing on and lying down on the warm, firm length of him. He pushes the loosened swim trunks impatiently down on Nicky's hips. Dick springing free, Nicky flushes with lust, half-hard already and clearly turned on in a big way by how Kyle always takes what he wants since he knows he can.

Kyle thrusts in a long, slow, rocking movement directly against Nicky's cock, one hand planted on the chair beneath them. Nicky moans as Kyle's narrow hips draw back in preparation to grind against him again. Eager to get his hands on what's right there undulating atop him, Nicky gets Kyle's skin-tight suit down in back to expose his ass. He grabs a double handful of it, urging Kyle on with the next thrust. The stilted movement is sharper, harder, and squeezes

Nicky's thick cock between their bodies with Kyle's dick still trapped in his bathing suit. Exhaling around a deep moan, Kyle dips his head to suck briefly at Nicky's lower lip. Nicky kneads Kyle's ass, using the handhold to pull him in harder. The thrusts start to come faster.

"Ever get fucked in a pool?"

"Mm-mm," Nicky grunts.

"Well, tonight's your lucky night," Kyle grins. Nicky spreads Kyle's cheeks and rubs with two fingertips through his crack and right over his hole. Pausing right there, Nicky brushes back and forth over the knot. Frowning, Kyle bites gently at Nicky's lip and rocks against his cock in shallow, firm pushes.

"Maybe it's yours," Nicky teases, breaching him with one fingertip, feeling Kyle's rim hug tightly around it. The small violation draws a soft, sweet gasp. Licking back over Nicky's lips, Kyle quiets further speculation with a deep kiss, filling Nicky with tongue, taking his breath away. He surges upward to get in farther, turning his head to the side. Nicky's head comes up off the cushion, chasing into the kiss. He takes control of it, tongue twisting with Kyle's, and inserts his finger a little deeper. It makes Kyle moan. Precome weeps from his dick which is now uncomfortably stiff and trapped in the too-tight suit.

"So fucking hot," Kyle sighs. He wrenches free and slides down Nicky's body to suck on his left nipple, which is a little bigger and much darker than Kyle's. Mouth watering, he hungrily seals his lips around the silken flesh in a kiss then pulls off to tease the stiffened nub with the tip of his tongue. He's too low for Nicky to be able to finger him any longer, which is just what Kyle intended.

"Playin' hard to get?" Nicky asks breathlessly.

Sliding even lower, Kyle grabs a condom off of the concrete. He tears it open with his teeth and starts to roll it onto Nicky. "Nah, I ain't hard to get," Kyle replies. "See?"

Sucking on the latex-sheathed cockhead, Kyle feels Nicky take hold of his face with both hands and try to thrust farther into his mouth. He's panting and moaning softly. Kyle loves it. This is exactly where he wants to be—taking Nicky apart, making someone happy, sharing a pure moment of undisguised passion. Kyle relaxes his throat and lets Nicky slide farther back over his tongue. The thick cock fills Kyle's mouth as it first pushes in, then slips right back out. Moaning around the taste of latex and the pulsing heat, Kyle gets lost in the decadent debauchery. He gives Nicky a slow, thorough, lazy blow-job. All that matters is sucking, licking, kissing and stroking Nicky's gorgeous cock, and Kyle loves that, too. Even more, he gets off on the stark honesty of it, that Nicky would do anything, drop whatever it is he's doing, make any excuse, tell any lie to get over here and let Kyle worship his incredibly hot body.

When Nicky is right on the edge, his balls drawn up tight, dick like hot iron and ready to shoot, Kyle strips off the condom. He indulges in some skin-to-skin contact before doing anything else, nuzzling against Nicky's cock, revelling in the silken feel of it sliding against his cheek. Burying his nose against Nicky's groin, inhaling the wonderful, rich scent, he ignores Nicky's breathless, whimpered pleading for a few seconds. Fondling Nicky's balls, Kyle tugs on them gently. Hooking the junction of his index finger and thumb around them, he guides the organ to his mouth and sucks one of the testicles.

"Oh, shit! *Kyle*," Nicky gasps, thrusting into the air, his fingers skating back over Kyle's scalp as he yanks Kyle's talented lips impossibly closer.

Humming, Kyle takes Nicky's member in hand and quickly brings him off after only a few strokes. With a shudder and a small cry, Nicky erupts. A thick jet of hot come splatters white over Nicky's light brown skin. Kyle smiles wickedly up from between Nicky's thighs, his lips slightly swollen and darker for the abuse they've taken. "So, can I fuck you now?"

"Yeah, whatever you want," Nicky agrees, nodding, trying to catch his breath. Kyle trails a hand through his spend, smearing it across overheated skin and taut muscle.

"Awesome. Get in the pool."

One of the reasons why Nicky makes such a great fuckbuddy for Kyle is that he's a naturally spectacular bottom. As much as he might try to get Kyle to give it up for once, when it comes right down to it, Nicky simply loves to get fucked. He doesn't even care about getting off, especially if he already has gotten off. He just relaxes into it and enjoys the hell out of the cock stuffing his ass full, which, in Kyle's humble opinion, is a beautiful thing.

Kyle gets Nicky comfortable in the water, giving him a fluffy, folded towel to hold between his chest and the unyielding lip of the pool's edge. He pulls Nicky's suit down to mid-thigh and enters him in a fluid, easy push once the prep is out of the way. Perfectly contented, Nicky keeps one arm wrapped around the towel and reaches back with the other in order to caress through Kyle's silky soft hair while Kyle moves inside him and drags open-mouthed kisses over the back of Nicky's neck.

The water slows everything down. Thrusts that may have been pointed and sharp are slowed and smooth. For what seems a long, long time, Kyle happily fucks a blissful Nicky. Making low, quiet sounds of pleasure, Nicky pushes his ass back onto each inward slide of Kyle's cock. Kyle's orgasm approaches steadily, hovering just out of reach for longer than it usually would, making the sex even better. He comes hard with a rough, loud grunt. Lip quivering, sweaty, shuddering, Kyle lets his chin rest atop Nicky's shoulder. After filling the condom, Kyle just floats there, sheathed completely in Nicky's incredible ass. His hips nudge and twitch against the rounded curve of Nicky's butt cheeks with each pulse as the aftershocks fry the remaining sense from Kyle's brain. He could stay just like that for hours, savoring the gentle *thump-thump-thump* of Nicky's heartbeat, the buoyancy of the pool's water, the hot grip around his cock, the chirp of crickets...

"Kyle! You here? KYLE!"

"Oh shit. Fuck. *Fuck*," Kyle hisses, instantly panicking. He pulls out, holding the condom on and yanking his trunks up to cover himself. Then he covers Nicky, too. "Shit. You gotta go. Out. Out of the pool. Quick!"

Dazed from the fucking, Nicky isn't quick on the uptake, but he's moved by the energy of Kyle's frantic commands. They vault out of the pool and Kyle wraps Nicky in the towel he's been clutching.

"Kyle!"

It's closer now, right at the outside of the gate.

With a groan of lament, Kyle sees how adorably lust-drunk Nicky looks, his eyes unfocused, water cascading in trickles from his lithe body and pooling at his feet. Kyle grabs Nicky's chin and hurriedly steals a quick kiss, humming at the luscious, warm taste of his lips. "Sorry. Go around the other way. Take the towel. I can't let him see you. Go. *Go*."

Kyle literally pushes him into action, spanking Nicky's well-fucked ass to get him moving. Nodding, Nicky goes, and jogs around the side of the property as the gate squeals upon opening.

"So hot," Kyle breathes, watching him disappear from sight. Hoarsely, without any concept of what he must look like and not really caring one bit, Kyle calls, "Yeah! Just a sec'!"

Though he's out of the water, Kyle still feels like he's moving in slow motion. His brain has somehow leaked out through his dick and left with Nicky. Crossing the yard, he finds himself standing in front of Darrek, still dressed in the stupid tuxedo.

"You're here," Kyle observes, stating the obvious. He hears what he's said and adds confusedly, "*Why* are you here?"

"Prom was lame," is all the explanation Darrek gives, but it's a good enough reason for Kyle who blinks up at him without surprise. Darrek seems to notice Kyle's very evident post-coital dishevelled bewilderment. "Holy shit. Were you just...? You were just fucking around, weren't you?! I heard another voice... and your face is red like..."

Kyle sees and feels Darrek do a thorough visual scan of his bruised-looking lips, flushed-dark nipples, dripping wet, overheated skin, tented swim trunks, and blissful, blank stare. The scrutiny makes Kyle's skin pebble with goosebumps.

"You're crazy," Kyle scoffs when Darrek doesn't stop staring. Then, giving himself away, he glances around to make sure they're alone.

Angering fast, maybe too fast, Darrek snaps, "Where is she?"

"Left."

"What do you mean, she left?"

"I mean, she left."

Kyle crosses to a patio table on which some clean towels are stacked. He takes one and dries his face. Suddenly, they both hear the soft sound of bare feet slapping on concrete behind Darrek and turn simultaneously toward it. Expression coloring with slightly exasperated anguish, Kyle sees Nicky approaching and quickly tries to gather his wits in order to come up with some kind of a cover story.

"Forgot my pants. Um, car keys," Nicky manages. "Hi."

Darrek stays mute, his jaw clenched and arms folded.

Kyle nervously scratches the back of his head, glancing around at the pool supplies and lotions on the tabletop for help or guidance and says, "Uh, this is… Tanner. He drove the girls over."

"Yeah, that's right," Nicky commiserates readily. He takes his clothes from Kyle who scoops them up and hands them over.

"I'll catch you later, okay?" Kyle says, holding Nicky's gaze. "Thanks for coming by."

"No problem. It was fun. Later."

Towering over both of them, utterly silent and radiating waves of unfriendly displeasure, Darrek bites his tongue as Nicky leaves. Kyle waits until he hears the car engine start and the crunch of tires rolling on the driveway before snagging his beer and retreating into the house.

"You fucking liar," Darrek accuses once they're both inside and the sliding glass door is shut behind them.

"How am I a liar?" Kyle retorts. "He drove Nicky over and brought a friend, too. We had a good time."

Feelings hurt in ways Kyle suspects he doesn't understand, Darrek bristles. "This why you didn't want to go with me to prom? You'd rather hang out with Tanner and some whores? Why did you even come over today?"

"Christ," Kyle sneers. "Got your panties in a twist, don'cha, Dare? I do have other friends. I'm allowed to have friends. I told you that prom isn't my scene. I came over today because I know it was a big deal for you. And why the hell are you here anyway? Shouldn't you be boning Sara in the back of a limo or in a scuzzy hotel room somewhere?"

Darrek is less than forthcoming with the answer. He bites it back for a good while before blurting, "She wasn't feeling well. I took her home."

Kyle laughs. "On the rag, huh? Damn. Bad luck for you. I hope she gave you a raincheck for the pussy at least."

The look on Darrek's face tells Kyle clearly enough that he has guessed right. That makes him laugh even harder. Shaking his head, he finishes his beer and goes to get another from the fridge. He brings back some bottled water for Darrek and shoves it into his hand.

"Here. Cool off. Calm the fuck down. It's not my fault you didn't score. Lemme get changed and we'll hang out, okay?" With an incredulous little head shake at Darrek's continued prissiness, Kyle walks past him and down the hall to his bedroom.

Darrek stands there, listening to Kyle's footsteps, drowning in an unbidden surge of blinding protectiveness. When he hears the soft sound of the bedroom door pushing open over thick carpet, Darrek instinctively turns and follows. Staying in the hallway, hidden in the deep shadows of the mostly unlit house, Darrek sees Kyle through the doorway as he peels off the damp swimsuit. Without thinking about what he's doing or why, just knowing that Kyle is his responsibility, sensing deception, afraid that Kyle is in more trouble than he's letting on, Darrek stays silent and still. He doesn't want Kyle to realize he's being observed because if Kyle thinks he's alone he's more likely to let down some of his behavioral walls.

There's a small bedside lamp on. It gives Darrek a good view when Kyle steps out of the wet trunks and tosses them underhand into the adjoining bathroom. His expression softened by perceived privacy, Kyle begins to remove the soiled condom.

Darrek stares guiltily but avidly at both the taboo sight of Kyle's flushed dark, come-soaked, half-hard cock lying cradled in a hand and at the beautiful sort of contentment on Kyle's face as he remembers intimacy with someone else, intimacy that Darrek knows he interrupted. It complicates an already muddled emotional response for Darrek. He's relieved that Kyle appears to be okay but strangely insulted by evidence that Kyle found happiness with someone else.

Covering his mouth with a hand, Darrek watches even more closely as Kyle gets a few wet wipes from a dispenser on his nightstand and cleans off his dick. There's no reflex to look away as Darrek observes his best friend like a predator. For Darrek it doesn't feel wrong or out of line for him to be moved to do what he's doing. On a deep level, beneath thought and logic, Darrek has always understood that this is his place, literally watching over Kyle, keeping him safe— from himself and others who would hurt him. Because Kyle is Darrek's. It's as simple as that. He always will belong to Darrek. Scrutinizing every inch of Kyle's bare body without his knowledge, Darrek makes sure he's healthy and unmarked. He's too preoccupied with a fleeting gladness that Kyle doesn't bear the sorts of bruises and marks that mar his own body to realize that he's suddenly completely hard.

Kyle goes into the bathroom and voids his bladder. There's a clear view from the hall if Darrek steps to the side a little. Taking his time, Kyle gets dressed, slipping on some boxers and a pair of jeans. He takes a moment to fix his hair in the mirror. In the darkness, Darrek waits, seeing everything. When Kyle appears ready to emerge, Darrek goes swiftly back to the den at the end of the hall and takes a drink from his water.

Kyle comes back out.

Darrek takes off his jacket, hanging it on the back of a chair, and asks, "So, was she tight?"

"Who?"

"*Nicky.*"

At first Kyle doesn't say anything. He just stares at Darrek with wonder, trying to read between the words and analyze the expression on Darrek's face. Darrek takes another drink. Kyle's eyes stay locked to him, letting his silence answer for him. It says plenty. Then, with a wry chuckle, Darrek's best friend and first love gives him a faint, honest smile and tells him, "You have no idea."

Divine Surrender

When Ben Knox discovers a clean-cut, blond, apparently-straight teenager named Kyle Roth in his office, looking for a professional Dominant, instinct draws him in. Since the exceedingly particular Kyle has already passed on Gabriel and Trace, Ben digs down beneath first impressions to expose Kyle's true motivations. Skillful as Kyle is at masquerading as the person the world expects him to be out of self-preservation, Ben has plenty of experience dealing with bruised souls. Kyle's bruises, though, go deep and the vulnerable darkness that Kyle tries to hide lures Ben in and takes them both farther than either is prepared to go. (M/M)

Chapter 1

Enslaving Goldilocks

While striding down Diadem's main hallway, Ben passed by the office and caught a glimpse of a young, sickeningly hot blond sitting in the chair across from the desk. After skidding to a halt long enough to rubberneck and frown quizzically at the stranger, Ben continued on to the main desk and Sam.

He barely had time to form a perplexed look and cock a thumb back in the direction of the office before Sam, Diadem's receptionist slash nurse slash friendly face, started in with an explanation. "There you are, Benny. You've got an appointment. Meet and greet for a potential new sub."

"The blond?" Ben said doubtfully. "Yeah, right." Raising his voice, he shouted for his good friend and fellow Dom, Gabriel Hunter, who had to be hiding around there somewhere, probably laughing his ass off, "Very funny, Hunter! I know you can hear me! What'd you do, bribe the pizza delivery boy?"

"Gabey's out back, hon," Sam told him. "The kid's legit."

Skeptical as ever, especially considering how Gabriel liked to rag on him constantly for going after guys too young and too pretty for Gabriel's tastes, Ben said, "There's no way. And since when do we do face-to-face meet and greets for new subs prior to a scheduled scene and paperwork and the rest of that bullshit?"

"Since now. This isn't his first time, either, just 'cause it's the first time you've seen him. Have a look through his file. It's on the desk. It's all in there. He already gave Trace and Gabe the thumbs down."

"No shit," Ben chuckled. "Why?"

Lowering her voice as much as possible for discretion, Sam whispered to him, "Trace's age is a trigger for him and he thought Gabe was too cold."

"Oh wow," Ben marveled, biting at his lip eagerly. He did love a challenge, especially when everyone else had failed miserably in the attempt. Pivoting on a heel, he headed right for the office, swinging around through the doorway, his hand clutching the frame.

When he reached the teenage-looking guy waiting for him, Ben stuck out a hand in greeting, saying, "Hey, how's it going? Nice to meet you, welcome to Diadem, the candyland of kinks, et cetera, et cetera."

They shook hands. Ben circled around behind the desk. He was glad he'd bothered to dress nicely that day. He was wearing grey pants, polished, heavy black boots, and a tailored, black shirt with the top three buttons undone. Add to that the fact that he'd recently taken a trip to the barber for a trim of his naturally curly, brown hair and was fairly militant about keeping his beard perfectly manicured, and he knew he looked *damn* good. It had to add a certain *je ne sais quoi* to his entrance for the precious, unsuspecting man-child awaiting him.

Lowering himself into the chair and spotting the paperwork right away, Ben flipped open the file and casually scanned the first page containing basics like name, address, and contact information before flipping to the second. Page two was a checklist of likes, dislikes and triggers as well as the notes made from previous visits with both Trace and Gabriel.

Goldilocks was watching him closely. The kid was wearing a non-descript pair of jeans and a white polo shirt with some well-cared-for work boots. He had bright blue eyes which were alert and intelligent as hell. He didn't appear intimidated at all but merely patient and maybe a little wary. Ben found it intriguing. He'd seen the burliest of Bears nearly piss themselves to be faced with one of Diadem's Doms for the first time. It was all kind of perfect, really. Trace was too old, Gabe was too cold. Maybe Ben would be just right. He started envisioning Goldilocks wearing a frilly apron—and nothing else—with pigtails in his hair as he tried out different sized dildos, different flavors of lube, and different types of spanking benches right before Ben, Trace, and Gabriel came upon the sweet little thing, ready to growl, snap, and tear into that ass.

He shook his head to clear it, pushing the fantasy away, hard. That shit was simply inappropriate. Tempting as fuck, but still inappropriate. At least until after the meet and greet.

"So," Ben started, letting the manila folder of neatly stacked letter-sized papers float back down to the desk. He glanced up at his visitor. "I'm Ben Knox. Maybe you knew that; maybe not. I'm still playing catch-up here. How are you? You good? Need a drink or anything?"

"I'm fine, thanks," Goldilocks replied softly. Even his voice sounded young—rough and raspy like he'd just given head for an hour straight, but young.

"You're fuckin' legal, right?" Ben murmured, sure they would have checked the kid's ID but wholly unconvinced he was old enough to be on the premises, let alone looking to get tied down, tortured and fucked silly. Bending the bottom edge of the folder's cover back, he scanned for a birth year in the personal details filled out in blue ink in neat, legible handwriting that slanted slightly to the left.

"I'm legal," Goldilocks reassured him. It was curious. One of the first things Ben had noticed on the paperwork was the little checked-off box indicating anal as one of Goldilocks' triggers. So, this potential submissive wanted to submit to a man, specifically, but didn't want to take a cock.

It didn't add up.

Why had the kid passed over Gabriel—even given the debatable coldness factor—when Gabriel had always refused to have sex with his submissives? It seemed a match made in heaven. Now they had a Dom who wouldn't fuck, and a sub who wouldn't fuck, and Ben stuck somewhere in the middle, loving to fuck and frustrated on all accounts.

Ben leaned forward over the desk to do a visual scan of the kid's face and body while the kid kept watching him with intense focus. Slender fingers tapped lightly away on the arm of the chair. There were cuts and bruises on those fingers, a sign, maybe, of a job doing manual labor. Maybe not. There were faint dark circles under his slightly bloodshot eyes and thin, long scars barely visible along the inside of his forearm.

"What are you looking for?" Ben inquired. "I mean, yeah, it's all here," he gestured to the papers laid out in front of him, which he had no further interest in. "But that's the official mumbo jumbo. I'll get a clearer picture of things if you would just kind of lay it out for me in your own words."

Goldilocks hesitated, but not because he didn't know what his answer was. Of that much, Ben was certain. They locked eyes and Ben felt himself being judged just as he was judging a potential client—and a young, troubled one at that.

After everything Ben had been through with Gabriel, Ben knew warning signs when he saw them, dancing and singing, flashing scars of both the mental and physical varieties. From the first moment Ben met Gabriel, it was like there was a big, neon sign above his head letting everyone know someone had taken too much, gone too far and left Gabriel in pieces. Just a glance at him—underage, gaunt, tormented, defensive, and humbly in need—would tell you, though he wasn't even an adult yet, he was already torn to shreds nonetheless. It had made Ben want to find whoever was to blame for that, and give back with fists, knives and pain what some son-of-a-bitch had taken from sweet Gabriel against his will.

For years, Ben had been angry about Gabriel, and for Gabriel. A lot of the decisions Ben made were influenced by that anger. It was a flame that would never burn down, and the light it cast formed weird shadows on everything he saw, forming demons where there might be nothing.

Sitting in that office, across from a potential new client, it wasn't the same as when he met Gabriel. There was no neon sign, blaring warnings. It was more like the crackle of electricity in the air, making hair stand on end. Some of Ben's internal alarms were going off, but he didn't know why. Not yet. One thing was certain—there were things beneath the surface with Goldilocks to watch out for. It was like detecting land mines buried just under the dirt near your feet. Best watch yourself unless you want to get something vital blown off.

"I'm looking for a Dom," Goldilocks answered with a no-nonsense tone, not shy or unsure in the slightest. "One who knows his shit and one whom I can trust. Someone who's not gonna bust my balls just for laughs or for another notch in his belt, but who'll give me what I need, because it's what he understands I'm unable to do on my own, without guidance, help, and a safe environment."

"And no sex," Ben said, filling in the obvious blank.

"Is that a problem?" Goldilocks didn't look like he cared if it was a problem. He'd simply move along to the next cottage and see what they had to offer instead.

"No. I can work around it. Are you straight?"

"Sometimes."

Ben's interest snagged hard on that.

"Have you ever submitted to another man before?"

"No."

"A woman?"

"No. Look, Mr. Knox, I might be new at this, but I know what I'm looking for, and that's a long-term arrangement with someone who's capable and trustworthy. I'm not here on a whim for a one-time thing because of some passing experimental phase. That's why I wanted to meet with you first. I need to know if this is going to work or not, before committing to anything."

Holy shit did this kid have a set of balls on him. Impressed, Ben got out of the chair. He walked around so that he was face-to-face with Goldilocks.

"Stand."

Blondie got to his feet slowly, a muscle flexing in his chiseled jaw, his pink, full lips pursing in concentration. Ben had an inch or two in height on the kid, which was good. He liked to be able to look down at his slaves. Taking hold of the kid's jaw, turning his face slightly to the side and caressing lightly down the side of his neck, down the front of his chest, Ben deliberately dragged the side of his bent finger slowly over Goldilocks' nipple, feeling it stiffen, and kept going lower. His crooked finger slid down to Blondie's waist. Pivoting his wrist, Ben dropped his hand lower still and, splaying his fingers wide, grabbed hold of the swell of Goldilocks' groin. A telltale shiver worked its way through the kid and his cheeks grew flushed. Gently, gradually, Ben began to knead his potential slave's cock through the denim of his jeans, feeling it respond quickly, swelling in his grasp.

Ben made a mental note or three. The kid got hard from being touched by a man. That was good. That was important.

It clearly wasn't the kid's first time, but the touching was affecting him strongly nonetheless. Ben couldn't decide if it indicated he was a virgin or not, but Ben would bet money the kid had never taken cock before. Blondie wouldn't make eye contact with Ben and kept his gaze lowered. His breathing quickened and he began making these endearing little gasps, while small frown lines formed in his brow.

More mental notes were tallied. Blondie was embarrassed to be fondled, and it played with his head. Maybe he was just looking for an outlet for his gay tendencies, a place to get off without the danger of some jerk trying to date-rape him at the end of the night.

"I'm glad you're enjoying that, Goldilocks," Ben said amiably, with a faint, crooked grin. He was getting turned on hard from all of the subtle cues he was getting and how much he sensed this kid wanted to submit to him and let Ben play with him. "Truth be told, I'm fuckin' enjoying it too. No sex while you're submitting, correct?"

"Correct," was the breathless, abrupt answer.

"But touching is okay?"

"Yeah. Yes."

"Can I slip a finger up your ass? A small toy?"

Goldilocks moaned behind his tightly sealed lips. Ben's cock throbbed with need. The opened office door called to him. Glancing sideways at it, Ben let go of his new plaything and went to close the door. He returned to his potential client and said softly, "Look at me, Kyle."

Startlingly blue eyes rose to meet Ben's gaze.

Playing on a hunch, he asked, "Is sex *outside* of the Dom/sub arrangement a possibility?"

Kyle licked his lower lip wet, then chewed on it, his gaze skittering back and forth between Ben's eyes. Ben continued to process all the information flowing his way.

"Depends."

"On what?"

"On if I can trust you."

"Scares you, doesn't it?"

"Yeah," Kyle admitted.

"Your paperwork says no penetration, but, fuck, I'd love to get inside you," Ben sighed. "But, since I'm not a rapist, no means no. That's an absolute. I won't do anything without your consent, even if I want to."

"I appreciate the honesty."

"Everyone who knows you thinks you're straight, don't they?"

Kyle nodded, said, "Yes."

"You've experimented enough to know you want this, but need to be with someone who you don't doubt will take care of you, who'll always play by your rules, and who you can be honest with about what gets you hard."

Exhaling heavily, eyes closing, Kyle seemed to fight some internal battle with himself, especially when Ben reached out and gave Kyle's erection a gentle squeeze through his tented pants. "Seems I make you hard."

"Please," Kyle moaned.

"If we do this," Ben started. "I have conditions."

"Okay."

"Hands behind your back. Eyes on me. Feet slightly apart."

Kyle shifted into position, his breathing growing heavier as Ben continued to fondle him through the straining fabric of his pants, a slight, somewhat beautiful frown appearing on his angelic face.

"No using the day of a scene," Ben said sternly. "No using the night *before* a scene. No using the night *after* a scene. You come to me healthy and sober or I send your ass home. No refunds. Understood?"

"Mm-hmm," Kyle grunted, chewing on his lower lip, looking caught.

"The response is, 'yes, Sir' or 'yes, Master', not 'mm-hmm.'"

"Yes, Sir."

"Good."

One of the most amazing things about this potential client was that other than the conditions regarding penetration and sex, there were almost no other restrictions on Kyle's forms—even the extreme shit that almost all of Ben's other subs checked off. Literally everything else was on the table, even possibly, if Ben played his cards right, getting a piece of that ass on an unofficial, hush-hush basis. It was too good to pass up. Way too good.

"If I think you're using after a scene, I will follow your hot ass home and check on you myself. If you agree to be mine, I take that seriously. You heed my rules or I'll make your life hell."

Kyle nodded, then muttered, "Yes, Sir."

"Louder."

"Yes, Sir!"

Ben chuckled, so eager to get Kyle into the dungeon, naked and willing. The hunger had teeth like knives, gnawing at his self-control.

"I would fuckin' love to be your Master. What do you say, slave? We got ourselves a deal?"

Slowly, Kyle smiled. His reticence seemed to fall away like a stuffy coat on a hot day. It just made Ben want to grab him and kiss him until he moaned some more.

And Kyle answered, "Yes, Sir. We do."

Chapter 2
Addicted

Still feeling the effects of Ben Knox's touch, Kyle walked down the hallway connecting Diadem's office to the reception area, passing a few doors on his left and a stairwell leading downward on his right. He tried to crane his neck and see what was below, as the stairs opened up on a room that was dimly lit and seemed to have a plain, concrete floor. Maybe that was the dungeon.

A few more steps found him passing the front desk, where Sam sat. She was nice enough, from what Kyle had seen. Sam was motherly, but not in a creepy or condescending way. Kyle pegged her at about thirty eight. She had shoulder-length light brown hair, an honest smile and seemed to be someone you'd want to grab a beer or five with and just shoot the shit for hours.

"All done with Ben?" she asked, looking him over in a way that spoke of both concern and curiosity.

"Yep. It went well. Might be seeing you again soon," he answered, smiling.

Folding her hands and resting her elbows on the desk in front of her, she smiled back and said, "That's great, hon. Gimme a call whenever you need to. We'll set you up."

"Will do. Bye."

"Drive safe."

The lobby had one middle-aged, grisly looking biker sitting in it. Wondering if he was there to see Ben or Gabriel, Kyle reached the front entrance and pushed through into the sunlight. Crossing the porch, he took the steps quickly, descending to the dirt of the parking lot and digging his keys out as he walked to his car.

It was strange how honesty had been taking a toll on him lately. It had become so second-nature to keep all of the things he truly cared and thought about, almost every minute of every day, entirely to himself. He owned his own home now, had a good job doing construction and buddies to hang out with at the end of a long week. He'd somehow attained his own piece of the American Dream. Of course, the house had been paid for out of his inheritance. The small, modest, cottage of a home had been easily procured when he'd put down half of the asking price in cash. The bank had overlooked the small factor of his age when presented with so much money up front, thanks to his good-for-nothing-else parents. They might not have been attentive or loving, but at least they'd given him the means to start living independently, on his own terms.

Never mind that he'd grown up in a white-collar home, but now lived a strictly blue-collar life, devoid of family or close friends. Never mind that the people he really wanted to talk to were the same ones that were the hardest to pick up the phone and call. Never mind that just getting out of bed some days took so much force of will that the only thing keeping him functioning wasn't gratitude or hope, but unquenchable fury and deep-seated, inescapable pain.

It was all just so fucking hollow. The pride he'd taken in establishing a new life for himself far away from everyone he'd ever known had carried him through the first year. But he was just as fickle as anyone else. Soon, it wasn't enough to have his freedom. The absence of a tangible threat to his mental or physical health wasn't enough to keep the nightmares away.

Jabbing the car key into the lock, getting the driver's side door opened, Kyle sat down behind the wheel with a sigh and marveled at how exhausting it could be to be somewhat honest for once.

Without much forethought, he got the car going and began to drive out of the secluded parking lot surrounding Diadem's main building, coasting over the bumpy dirt road, flanked by tall, waving grass. Once he was back on asphalt, reflexes took over. The drive itself was mostly muscle memory as thoughts of Ben's smile, his blue eyes and fiery attitude lingered long after their meeting was through.

Twenty minutes later, he was in an urban, run-down section of the neighboring town. Tall, brick townhouses, some with boarded-

up windows, most with heaps of junk piled on front porches, brack-
eted the road. Carving a path through the street lined with cars and
people with no thought about wandering out into traffic at random
intervals to cross, Kyle looked for the number he wanted. He saw the
black digits nailed above the porch — 567 — and pulled over where he
could. Locking the car up and checking the handle for good measure,
he glanced around, saw lots of folks with enough on their own minds
to bother giving a shit about him, and hurried up to the house's side
door.

There was a cracked fixture above it, and the bulb gave off a yellow light, meant to keep the bugs away. The door's screen was torn in
three places and the frame was hanging on by one rusty hinge. Raising his fist, he knocked twice, then stuffed his hands in his pockets,
palming the folded bills he'd tucked in there. It was another habit
rather than premeditation. It made him feel more at ease to at least
have the cash on him, just in case.

There was movement inside the old house, a shifting of shadows
and the sound of footsteps descending stairs. A chain rattled as someone on the other side of the door fiddled with the locks. One, two,
three of them were released. The door inched open and a beady eye
peered out from under lank hair.

"Hey," Kyle murmured. "You got stuff?"

"What d'you need?" was the mumbling reply.

"I've got fifty. Lookin' for the good stuff; not that shit you gave
me last week."

"Fifty?"

"Yeah."

The door closed again. Kyle sighed and heard more movement
and rustling within. He tried to be patient, knowing that Branden
didn't typically have his act together. Everything he did was like
moving through water, slowing him down, causing plenty of drag on
his body and mind.

Finally, the door reopened, a little wider this time. Branden shook
his ashy brown hair from his eyes, leaning against the doorway as
he held out a closed fist. Kyle stuffed the bills in Branden's fist as he
simultaneously palmed the vial tucked within.

The door closed heavily. Kyle hurried back to his car.

A guilty sort of exhilaration charged him up as he drove a little faster on the way home. He was barely in his driveway before he had the car parked and the vial in his hands. Twisting the cap off, he tapped some of the white powder onto a knuckle and breathed it in with a sharp inhale.

The rush went right to his head, like bubbles in soda soaring upwards, popping at the surface.

"Fuck yeah. Holy *shit...*" he moaned, body sagging back into his seat.

As key ties holding his mind together slowly became unraveled, he saw in his memory that contract. It was all there. His name, his information, his preferences and lack of boundaries—except one—were all there in black and white, undeniable. There was something pure about that, having it all written down, tucked in a manila folder and placed on the desk of a cocky, hard-bodied, big-dicked Dominant who hadn't hesitated in grabbing hold of Kyle's cock to see how he'd react. God, he couldn't wait. As formal and safe as it was to submit to a Dominant in a professional setting, as the result of a business arrangement between consenting adults, it was also unspeakably dangerous, especially for someone like Kyle.

But when he was with Ben, Kyle wouldn't have to put on an act like he did with the other, very hetero guys on his construction crew. He wouldn't have to pretend to care if a hot woman walked by or flirt with anyone he had no intention of hooking up with, just for show. He could be focused on his male Dom and not be ashamed of their interactions. It was private. Ben would be discreet.

Even at Diadem, though, there were some key cards he had no intention to show. Sure, he'd tell Ben, or whomever, the answers to their pointed questions. He'd obey and be respectful. He wouldn't go behind their back or try to get away with anything. It was all straightforward. But, it wasn't everything.

The edges of Kyle's awareness burned away, focusing him right down the middle. Parts of his reality melted away while others came into crystal-clear focus. He needed to get inside, ride out the high in a better place than the driver's seat of his car.

Good for Ben for spotting the signs. It didn't make a difference to Kyle. He had no intention to stop using, no matter how much of a tough guy Ben thought he was. Some things merited the distractions and relief that came with chemical alterations. Walking up to his front door, as cool, fresh air ghosted over the back of his neck, he just enjoyed the slow build of fuzziness and calm, pushing the pain that was always with him, a part of him, slightly out of range.

He reached for the doorknob, and caught sight of the inside of his left forearm. The self-made cuts on his arms and legs had mostly healed. That was intentional. He'd waited until they weren't fresh to initiate the process of going to Diadem. Now that he'd signed the papers to begin meeting with Ben on a regular basis, Kyle knew he had to stick to his resolve to lay off the knives and razorblades for a while.

His thoughts strayed to one of the places they seemed to perpetually linger lately, wondering about his best friend, Darrek, wondering if he was okay, and wondering if he wondered if Kyle was okay. Luckily, the drugs pushed the heartache back, too. Seeing his blood run red over the gleaming, silver edge of a sharp blade would push it farther, but that wasn't a weapon he could wield any longer. He needed something stronger. He needed Ben.

Kyle was a mind-fuck from the start. Everything about him screamed All-American jock playing straight for appearances sake, while what he really wanted was another guy touching his cock, maybe spanking his ass and telling him what a bad boy he was. But there were other facets, too. Like those scars on his arm, signaling to Ben that the kid was a cutter. There was also the fact that the kid was a junkie. Now, how *much* of a junkie he was, was still up for debate. Was he a cokehead? Weed freak? Was he into pills or, god forbid, meth or heroin? He didn't seem too far gone. If he could follow Ben's rules about using in the lead-up or come-down from a scene, maybe it was manageable. Ben had nothing against recreational drug use. There were countless times he'd hung out with Gabriel, passing around a joint, getting as high as the moon. But, there was a time and place. The only addiction Ben wanted Kyle to have was to Ben's cock, Ben's orders, and Ben's every whim.

As soon as Trace and Gabriel learned the news that picky-choosy Kyle Roth had signed the papers to be Ben's submissive, they started to rag on Ben for it. It seemed like Ben had become the bitch of some prude, stoner trash with a pretty face and a tight ass Ben was barely allowed to touch.

On the way back to their trucks after a long night at work, Ben saw Gabriel hesitate. Standing in the dirt beside his Discovery, the mosquitoes trying to eat them alive, Gabriel asked him, doubtfully, "You're really taking that Roth guy on?"

"Why not?" Ben countered, leaning back against his truck and shooing away the insects with a scowl. "He's a client. This is my job. He's hot. What's not to like?"

"He's an addict," Gabriel said heavily, with raised eyebrows and lips quirked with disapproval. "He's into self-harm. He gets touchy if you cross certain lines. He's not worth it."

"Yeah, well, not your problem, is it?" Ben stepped closer to Gabriel, slipping his hands into his pockets as he strolled over, looking up and down Gabriel's body. Funny how Gabriel, who was too pretty for his own good, just like Kyle, and had plenty of secrets, just like Kyle, had such a problem with those aspects of Kyle's identity. It was funny in a soul-rotting, tragically awful way, but funny nonetheless. "Come on, be honest, Hunter. You're jealous. He didn't like you. He likes me. And hey, you like me, too."

"Not *that* much," Gabriel retorted, looking pouty. He turned his back on Ben, but not before he gave Ben the tell-tale, fuck-me-Benny, once-over glance that always had Ben's dick instantly standing up and taking notice. Gabriel opened his driver's side door and let out a small, sexy sigh of complaint as Ben snaked an arm around his waist. He palmed Gabriel's stomach and kissed a spot under his right ear, watching avidly as Gabriel's eyes closed in what looked like delirious pleasure. The smell of Gabriel's aftershave was still there, under the more intoxicating scent of his skin. Scraping his teeth, briefly, over the side of Gabriel's neck, Ben fondly recalled the last time he'd been permitted to map with the tip of his tongue, every plane, curve and contour of Gabriel's body that never saw the light of day.

"Anytime, anyplace, Gabey," Ben whispered. "You know the drill."

"Raincheck," Gabriel murmured, pulling away and closing the door on Ben before another word could be spoken.

"Yeah, what else is new?" Ben murmured, watching as Gabriel reversed out of his spot and drove away, kicking up a cloud of dirt behind him as he hurried home to Trace. For half of a second, Ben wondered if Gabriel would be sneaking into Trace's bed that night or not, looking for an orgasm spiked with a smidge of dub-con. He'd bet on not, but you never knew with Gabriel. He could surprise you sometimes.

With Diadem dark and empty behind him, Ben pushed thoughts of Gabriel and Trace's equally complicated relationship away and got in his truck. He was starving, but the thought of heading home to an empty house was kind of depressing. His other options weren't that great either though. He could go eat somewhere alone or with strangers, or he could call someone up and invite himself over. Sitting in the cab of his truck, he delayed making a decision for a few minutes, liking the quiet and the dark of the night. The stars were out over the fields surrounding Diadem's barn, located at the rear of the property. Beyond it, the tree line was a jagged, black line swallowing everything the starlight couldn't touch. Bats swooped at terrifying speeds, snagging food from mid-air. Insects sang. A plane twinkled in the sky, almost too small to see as it flew overhead.

His thoughts circled back around to the conversation with Gabriel. Even if Gabriel and Trace made comments about Kyle, Ben didn't pay any attention. It was a matter of opinion and perspective. You couldn't judge people on what they seemed to be. Ben's love for Gabriel said as much. When someone came into your life, laden with the baggage of homelessness and a long history of abuse, it was easy to be tempted to shelve them in certain categories. Ben had done Gabriel the favor of giving him the benefit of the doubt, treating him the way Ben would want to be treated, in his place. He'd always seen Gabriel for the kind of friend he was, and how diligently he worked to find a better path for himself, rather than the product of tragic circumstances. Ben could give Kyle the benefit of the doubt too. More than that, he understood why Gabriel was, perhaps, not yet able to give Kyle as much as Ben could.

When Kyle fucked around with guys, it was all about getting off. He was always in charge. Picking guys who were younger or less experienced helped. Those hook-ups were usually just grateful to have someone good looking willing to touch or suck their dick and didn't care where Kyle drew the line. It was hard to find someone else who was gay, and willing. Physical attraction was a bonus. Whether or not Kyle let his partners fuck him was irrelevant.

He never let them fuck him. *Kyle* did the fucking.

He'd actually had sex with so many guys, he'd lost count. His partners had been tall, short, heavy or stick-thin, black, white, Asian, and Hispanic. It didn't matter. Kyle wasn't overly picky. As long as they were male, and around his age and weren't a monster looking to ruin his life, Kyle was cool with whatever.

"I'm seeing a new guy today," he said, settling more deeply into the couch. "His name is Ben. He doesn't know how much of a hot mess I am. Or maybe he has an idea, but doesn't know specifics. But really, no one but me and my bestie knows specifics, and actually even *he* doesn't *remember* specifics, so that leaves just me I guess. Anyway, I don't dwell on the past anymore. I'm looking forward. Ben's forward."

"Tell me more about Ben," his shrink invited, jotting notes on her tablet.

"He's not stupid, or evil. I like him. It'd be good if it worked out with him. I've been really... I don't know. Lonely?"

"Ben is someone you're romantically interested in?"

"Ooh, loaded question!" Kyle grinned. "We'll see. I haven't decided yet."

"So he's a friend?"

"No way," Kyle laughed. "He's just new. We have a deal."

"And how do you feel about that?"

"Great," Kyle shrugged. "Nervous. Nervous but great."

Checking his watch, Kyle figured he had an hour and a half before he had to be at Diadem, washed and shaved and thoroughly mentally prepared for just about anything.

"I'm not good with letting other people call the shots. I'm gonna try letting Ben call some, see how it goes. Maybe it'll be progress. Anything's gotta be an improvement on the way things are now, right?"

"You're referring to the loneliness you've been experiencing since moving here?"

"Yeah. No, you're right. Guess it could be worse. That was overstating it. It might be more accurate to just say that I hope things keep getting better. Maybe that's greedy, but... I don't know. That'd be nice. I don't have the greatest track record of trusting people who aren't going to be bad for me in the long run. Everyone's gotta luck out once in a while though. I think I'm due for some luck."

Memories clouded his mind. Closing his eyes, Kyle took a deep breath and opened them again. His doctor was analyzing him, or trying to. There was a lot he'd never say, even to her. But it was good to talk through things.

Checking his watch again, he saw the minutes draining away. His pulse quickened and butterflies in his stomach made him feel queasy. No turning back now.

Chapter 3
Slave Versus Master

Their first BDSM scene was just between Ben and Kyle, in the sub-level dungeon of Diadem. Ben didn't want any distractions—no assisting from the other Doms. He wanted to get a better idea of what he was dealing with. It was about building trust and a connection with Kyle. It had to be just the two of them.

Ben could tell Kyle was smart, and was glad he was. It made the challenge to tame and subdue him that much more fun. He would much rather dominate an intelligent, willful slave, than a weak-willed, stupid one.

For Kyle's comfort, Ben scheduled their appointment for seven in the evening on a Friday when Trace and Gabriel were both due to be away from Diadem. It was after the workday hours, so there would be no conflict with Kyle's job, and he would have the whole weekend to recuperate. Ben waited in the dungeon for Kyle to arrive. Once Kyle had made his way past Sam at the front desk and came downstairs, he walked slowly and tentatively into the large, open space and toward Ben. He was wearing a jacket, his car keys jingling in the pocket as he fiddled nervously with them.

"Come on. A little closer. A little closer," Ben beckoned.

Kyle was looking everywhere, at everything, checking out the furniture and gear on display, his eyes wide with amazement and apprehension.

"There are hooks on the wall for your things," Ben told him, indicating the spot. "Take off everything but your underwear, then get your ass over here."

Somewhat awkwardly, fumbling and hopping on one foot as he

pulled off his boots and struggled with his shirt, Kyle undressed. Ben was wearing a pair of snug-fitting black pants and heavy motorcycle boots wrapped with wide straps. He wasn't wearing a shirt, so the muscles of his chest and chest hair were on display. His upper arms were wrapped in wide, black leather straps just like his boots. Ben was going the extra mile in every sense to impress and intimidate appropriately. When Kyle looked at him, Ben wanted him to think of sex, not business. He had quite a few years' worth of experience on Kyle, and wanted Kyle to sense that.

He watched, salivating, as Kyle crossed to him. Kyle was the All-American young man—slim, toned, tan, magazine-pretty, barefoot and clad in only a pair of low-rise white briefs. The only thing in Ben's mind was hope that he could get his new, straight-acting, chaste slave to suck his cock that night before Kyle could chicken out. There was a lot, in fact, that Ben wanted to do to his slave or order his slave to do to *him*.

But, fuck, Kyle was hot. Though it was quite trimmed down, Ben had to admit Kyle's body was in great shape, with defined cuts of muscle in the V of his pelvis, his torso tight and muscular in a natural way from performing regular manual labor rather than going nuts in the gym. Fine, golden hair covered his arms and legs, begging to be caressed. His skin was sun-kissed and his eyes looked somewhat less bloodshot than the first time they'd met. The best part, though, was how instinct told Ben this was all so very new to Kyle, and seeing how shy it made him. Kyle didn't seem like a naturally shy person, but here, in Ben's dungeon, stripped down and voluntarily yielding all sexual power to Ben, Kyle was profoundly out of his element.

"Right here, slave," Ben commanded gently, pointing to a spot directly in front of where he stood. Was his heart racing, Ben wondered? Was he quivering? The temperature of his skin rising? Kyle stopped where Ben indicated, then tilted his head way back as he looked up at the chains hanging from the ceiling as well as the shackles attached to the ends. "What's your safeword?"

"Varese."

"Hmm. Interesting choice. Sam is the only other person in the building, but she'll be here the whole time. She's a former nurse and she'll be listening in, for your safety and comfort."

"Good. Okay," Kyle sighed, visibly relaxing a little. "Thanks."

"Now, my job as your Master is to respect you, as I expect you to respect me. Since we don't know each other very well yet, we'll go slow. It's crucial for you to be able to trust me completely. We good so far?"

"Yeah," Kyle nodded, watchful and alert as ever. His arms were folded self-consciously over his chest, his posture somewhat slumped out of self-consciousness, and his nipples stiff, though the air in the room was warm. When his gaze kept flicking up to the shackles dangling overhead, Ben saw him curl in on himself even more, hiding as much as he could as long as he was able.

"You're to address me only as Master or Sir. That means you say, 'yes, Sir,' 'thank you, Sir,' and so on. Mind your manners."

"Yes, Sir."

"You up for a little bondage, slave?"

"Yes, Sir," Kyle answered somewhat meekly, almost with a question mark at the end of his answer, glancing up again at the shackles.

"Awesome," Ben said eagerly. "Stretch your arms up above your head."

After a heavy exhale, Kyle slowly did as asked. Ben fastened Kyle's wrists into the leather shackles, making them tight enough that he couldn't slip out, but not tight enough to cut off circulation. Then, he tightened the slack on the chain, drawing Kyle's arms up even more, stretching him out. It lengthened his spine, pulling him up to his full height, his feet not quite flat on the floor.

Ben could see Kyle's chest rising and falling as his breathing quickened. Drawn up to the balls of his feet, Kyle realized quickly how his range of movement had been severely restricted. Every part of him grew tense and clenched. Each golden hair on his body stood upright as his flesh pebbled.

"Okay. Okay. Okay," Kyle was murmuring softly to himself. After a moment, as Ben circled around him, drinking in the sight of every inch of exposed skin, every muscle tight and expecting his touch, Kyle closed his eyes and tried to regulate his breathing. That was a good sign. Ben was glad Kyle knew to do that without being asked.

As the seconds drew into minutes, Ben knew Kyle could feel him staring at his suntanned skin flushing pinker. His hands curled into fists. His dick was not quite soft inside those little white briefs. Oh, how Ben hoped Kyle had a fetish for being displayed.

Going to the wall, Ben sought and turned a knob. Instantly, water began to sprinkle down onto Kyle from above. The water trickled down his body, collected at his feet and went out through a discreet drain in the floor. The temperature should have been warm, and the air in the dungeon was set to be warmer than usual as well, to keep Kyle from shivering too much.

"Fuck. Oh fuck," Kyle moaned softly. His golden hair grew damp, hanging in wet tendrils over his eyes. His only article of clothing — the briefs — became soaked. Soon, they were transparent and clung to his dick and the rounded muscles of his ass.

Retrieving a pair of latex gloves, Ben made sure Kyle could see him getting ready. It caused Kyle's breathing to quicken even more, his rosy lips parted around soft gasps. Water dripped prettily from Kyle's eyelashes, lower lip, chin, the end of his nose, and those blond tendrils of hair.

Speaking slowly and deliberately, standing in front of Kyle, only inches away, Ben tugged on the gloves and asked, "Would you like me to touch your cock, slave?"

The word 'cock' drew a pleasant shiver. As if in answer, Kyle's dick twitched inside the clinging briefs.

"I'm waiting."

"Yes, Sir. Please, touch me."

"Touch you where?" Ben asked leadingly.

"Please touch my cock."

"Manners."

"*Sir.*" Kyle made a soft little growl of frustration and embarrassment, then tried again. "Please touch my cock, Sir."

"Better," Ben grinned. He made a point of staring right at Kyle's dick, letting the moment draw out. The longer he looked, the more Kyle squirmed and the more erect he became. Before Ben's eyes, Kyle's dick grew stiffer, redder, thicker, and Kyle couldn't stay still. As he became undeniably aroused, he pulled at the chains, drew up on his toes, let his head fall forward, then turned his face toward his arm, breathing heavily against the skin there as water coursed down around his mouth. It was a hell of a sight.

"Kind of unconvincing, though," Ben *tsk*ed, shifting a little closer, so that Kyle could feel his body heat. "Try again. Ask me."

"Fuck," Kyle groaned. "Please touch my cock, Sir."

"You like it when I look at your cock, don't you, slave?"

Another shiver. Ben could practically taste the pre-come dripping from Kyle's slit.

"Yes, Sir."

"How much do you like it?"

"A lot, Sir," Kyle grimaced, seeming angry with himself.

Moving around to Kyle's side, Ben reached for him as Kyle tracked him with sharp watchfulness. Covering his slave's erection with his entire, gloved left hand, Ben felt the heat of him. Wrapping his fingers around the stiffened, swollen shaft through the soaked cotton, Ben added some pressure to his grip and, with his thumb only, began rubbing over the plum-shaped head. Kyle hummed, frowning heavily. When Ben's squeeze became a stroke, down to his root, back up to squeeze around his bulbous cockhead, the hum shifted into a purr.

A fucking *purr*.

The sound of it nearly made Ben come in his pants. It put iron in his cock like very few things did. Just like that, his supreme goal suddenly became provoking that sound again, and as often as possible.

Growing impatient, wondering, with so much lust it physically hurt, if he could make Kyle purr while he sucked on his new Master's cock, Ben gave up pretense and shoved his hand inside the flimsy briefs that no longer hid anything. Once he had a handful of Kyle's bare flesh, Ben stroked him with tight, long, complete strokes until Kyle was rocking against his fist, counter to every tug. He guided Kyle's hot, thick cock upright and left it pointed upward, trapped under the elastic band of his underwear with only his reddish-purple cockhead exposed. Water trickled down Kyle's body and over it. It took every bit of Ben's will to not get down on his knees and taste that. Most of all, he wanted to trace the divot in Kyle's crown with the tip of his tongue and tease the tiny opening just to see what kind of noises he would make.

"Good fuck, I'm gonna enjoy this little arrangement of ours," Ben sighed.

"Thank you, Master," Kyle murmured softly.

"Mm, say that again," Ben moaned, moving his thumb back and forth over Kyle's slit, using gentle friction to stimulate the spot.

"Thank you, Master," he repeated, adding a little spice to the words like he was *trying* to make Ben crazy.

Ben had to get it together. He really was becoming Kyle's bitch and they'd barely started. It was time to take the power back.

Shifting around to stand behind Kyle, Ben hooked a finger in Kyle's insignificant underwear and drew them down to hug under the curve of his pristine, deliciously fuckable ass—the kind they made statues and paintings of in tribute.

"Jesus Christ," Ben heard himself hiss. Goosebumps pebbled his skin as his hand caressed up Kyle's back, through the rivulets of water, over heated skin and tensed muscle. He took hold of him by the back of the neck and watched as Kyle clenched his ass and drew up on his toes, his calf muscles tensing beautifully. "This? Is mine. No one else's. Not even yours. It's fuckin' *mine*. You hear me, slave?"

"Fuck yes, Sir," Kyle rasped.

"God damn."

Ben caressed back down the side of Kyle's back, along the slight dip of the small of his back, over the rounded muscle of his ass. He knew what he needed to do. He took a few steps toward the wall to turn the water off, then came right back to Kyle. Already, Kyle was starting to shiver though the heat in the room was cranked up. Ben crouched down behind him and palmed Kyle's ass with one hand cupping each cheek. Then, he spread him open. One fingertip quested over and rubbed directly over his hole.

Kyle grunted. The sound broke free and shattered.

Leaning forward, Ben scraped his teeth over Kyle's left cheek, then sucked a kiss to the heated, damp skin, tasting him for the first time. He realized, then, that he was breathing hard, too.

Kyle tried to tense up but Ben held him open, rubbing gently over the nervously clenched ring of muscle, teasing it until it grew pink and blood began to beat under the skin.

Ben let go and stood. He came around to Kyle's front and saw how hard he was, the way he was gasping, his parted lips quivering, his gaze lowered submissively. There was no decision. Suddenly, Ben was just kissing him. Then Kyle's tongue was in his mouth. Ben pulled Kyle's entire body against him, palming his incredible bare ass, grinding against his hard-on, nipping at his lower lip, and tongue-fucking him breathless.

They broke apart and Kyle's pupils were blown black with lust.

"Please, Master, let me suck you."

"Oh *hell* yes," Ben moaned.

Who the fuck cared if he was letting Kyle choose how this played out? If it made Kyle feel more comfortable with Ben and got Ben a blowjob, then he was all for it. The shackles were opened, Kyle's arms released.

He fell to his knees, working open Ben's pants with frantic, fumbling fingers. Ben grabbed a condom from a tray of supplies nearby and tore the wrapper open, rolled the rubber on as Kyle licked his lips and stared at Ben's cock like he was starving for it.

With a growl, Ben let Kyle guide him back between his lips and into his mouth. Kyle closed his flushed, hot lips, gave him suction and took him deeper than Ben expected with a hum of pleasure.

"Hands off. Touch yourself," Ben ordered.

Right away, Kyle started to masturbate, pulling his cock out, tugging at it with a rapid pace while Ben rode Kyle's tongue and lips. The sight of that red, fat cock, slipping again and again through Kyle's fingers drove Ben crazy. He plunged in to the hilt, lodging in Kyle's throat, holding him there as the muscles of his throat worked around his girth. It was unbelievably good. Ben pulled back and kept taking, fucking Kyle's mouth hard and fast. And Kyle could take it. His eyes rolled back in ecstasy and he started to purr. The purring seemed to build to a climax. Staring down at Kyle, Ben noticed how Kyle had his left hand held behind him, resting obediently against the small of his back while his right pumped his dick at a frenzied speed and Ben had to wonder, *Good fuck, how had Kyle never done this before?*

Ben came with a startled, breathless cry, shuddering. With wide licks and open-mouthed, filthy sucks, Kyle worshiped Ben's cock as he came down and Ben fell farther than he ever had before.

Kyle stopped touching himself without being asked.

"Please, touch my cock, Master," he begged from his knees, his lips darker now and slightly swollen from being roughly used, his voice breaking over the words.

Ben pulled him to his feet, pushed him backward a few steps to the wall. When Kyle had turned around and had his hands splayed on it, bent forward, legs kicked apart with Ben's feet, Ben pressed himself up against Kyle's back, fitting his sheathed cock between Kyle's cheeks. Then he reached around and began to tug Kyle's cock with long, slow strokes from root to tip.

After a few strokes, Kyle was shouting, his voice hoarse. Ben rocked slowly against him, grinding against Kyle's ass counter to the tugs at his dick. Kyle came with a whimper, convulsing subtly in Ben's embrace while Ben pressed kisses over Kyle's shoulder and neck.

And Ben knew Kyle was his, even before Kyle again fell to his knees, turned around to face Ben. He buried his face in Ben's hip, wrapped his arms around Ben's body and held him, gasping, "Thank you, Master." The surprising amount of sincere gratitude in those three little words left Ben feeling like he didn't know up from down or right from wrong, like this young kid had showed up with his own rules and was praising Ben for being able to follow them. Simply put, Ben was dumbstruck.

Kyle used the showers to wash up and Ben stayed in the dungeon, cleaning up, then just sitting in a metal folding chair with a closed fist pressed against his lips, his expression reflecting his shock and alarm. They didn't speak as Ben walked Kyle upstairs to sit in a recovery room with some water to sip.

After a little while, Ben cleared Kyle to go.

"When can I come back?" Kyle asked.

Ben scanned his memory of his schedule. "Monday?" he answered.

"I can be here at eight," Kyle offered.

"It'll be... more intense... next time," Ben warned. "I won't go easy on you like I did tonight."

"Good," Kyle said with a grin, his eyes lighting up. "Bring it."

Chapter 4
Playing Games

"How did it go?" Gabriel asked the next day. It was around noon. Time to report for work and get the fun started.

"Fine," Ben answered shortly, digging his keys out of his pocket.

"Just fine? Why do you have that look on your face? Something happen with the kid?"

"Nope."

"Give me more than that, asshole," Gabriel laughed, nudging Ben's shoulder. Ben unlocked Diadem's main entrance and reached for the light switch.

"I'm still figuring him out," Ben said elusively, not wanting or able to put into words what his true reaction to Kyle was. Truth be told, it scared Ben how much he'd enjoyed dominating Kyle, not that there'd been much dominating at all. It was more fondling and sucking and coming than anything else.

"Did you spank him? CBT? Nipple play? Did he come? Did *you* come?"

Ben laughed breathlessly, shaking his head. "Shackled him under the sprinkler. He got off on being displayed and he was… he was really fucking hot, okay?" Ben threw up his hands in surrender. "He tasted like rainbows and he gave head like he'd gotten a degree in blowjobs from Boytoy University and his fucking ass is a thing of miracles. Okay? Ya happy now? Fuck."

"Jesus, Benny," Gabriel laughed. "That bad? Wow."

"Leave me alone, I'm confused," Ben complained.

"Yeah, sucks to be happy, doesn't it?" Gabriel teased, walking away to turn on more lights, throwing Ben a smile over his shoulder.

"Yeah, but not as much as Goldilocks," Ben murmured.

It was like Ben knew what Kyle needed, without having to be told why. That first scene went so well, it scared Kyle half to death. Afterward, he went home to his empty house, feeling more alive and content than he ever had before. His blood was pumping, his heart was at ease. He didn't have anything to fear, except what was already in his own head.

Ben's desire had been tangible. Even as Kyle parked his car and walked up to the door of his little house, the motion sensor light kicking on as he passed in front of the garage, he could still feel Ben's touch, his lips and the weight of his steely cock, nestled in the crease of Kyle's ass. Provoking desire in other men had never been an issue for Kyle. Though he was still just a teenager, Kyle knew how dangerous and intoxicating it was to be wanted.

Kyle found his house key and unlocked the door. Inside, the cozy, two-bedroom house was empty and dark. The curtains and blinds were all closed. Other than the humming of the refrigerator, it was silent as the grave. Maybe, to someone else, it would have been eerie to walk into such a dark place, alone, but Kyle had grown up alone. His parents had always been away, working, or busy. Every day after school, he came home to a lifeless house. More often than not, he was left to make himself dinner. He would eat alone, without company, unless he thought to invite someone over or tried to take advantage of his friends' parents' hospitality. Now that he was officially a self-sufficient adult and a property owner at such a young age, he'd grown comfortable living the same way he always had. It would have been stranger to actually come home to life and light instead of nothingness.

He set his keys on the table by the door. They clinked softly, a tiny sound in the silence. Then, his feet carried him to the stairs and up them to the second floor and the bathroom beyond the landing. In the mirror over the sink, he caught his reflection, and stopped to study it.

His naturally blond hair hung long over his forehead, almost obscuring his vibrantly sky-blue eyes. His features were the perfect blend of his father's masculine bone structure and his mother's striking features, leaving Kyle with a handsome appearance which had carried him far in high school, where it was the superficial which made the most difference. As a young adult and a carpenter, it sometimes hindered him. People who'd known him growing up expected a pretty-boy rich kid like him to be afraid to get his hands dirty and work hard. No one back home was ever willing to give him the benefit of the doubt, so that had been another perk of moving so far away. Here, he had no past. No one knew he came from money. Maybe he still looked like he couldn't handle himself, so the burden fell on him to put in the effort to transcend others' first impressions. Even with Ben, Kyle knew he saw Kyle's attractive, youthful exterior and, before they'd even exchanged words, tried to shelve him as something less than what he felt he was.

Kyle wasn't just a boy.

He wasn't privileged, either. Nature and fate hadn't done him any favors.

The bags and dark circles, just visible under his eyes, spoke of his demons. The slightly drawn, hollow look of his face hinted at an overly stressful, unhealthy lifestyle though his body clearly spoke to his physical fitness.

In a lot of ways, he was a walking contradiction.

Leaving his reflection behind, Kyle went to his bedroom and flicked on the wall switch to turn on the bedside lamps. It was a lonely place. Even when he was hooking up with someone, it was never at his house. No one ever reached the level of 'home visit worthy'. His bedroom was sacred. It was his space, most of all, above all other areas of the house. The bed was large; king-sized, like the one he'd grown up with, not that he needed that much bed. He only really used one edge of it. A single bed would have fit more nicely in the room, but he'd had bad experiences with smaller beds. Bigger was better in a lot of different ways.

He opened the nightstand drawer, and stuck his finger in a strategic place near the corner, reaching under a thick BDSM for Beginners manual he liked to thumb through when he couldn't sleep. The false bottom pulled up and he fished out a baggie containing four little pills. The baggie was sealed tightly. Palming the plastic, he set the drawer's false bottom back in place, slid the drawer back into the nightstand and climbed onto the bed.

Crawling to the center of the mattress, he sat cross-legged there with the baggie set in front of him. He arranged the pills without opening the bag, lining them up neatly in the exact center of the bag, as he was in the bed. The silence of the home wrapped around him like a blanket. The whole house was his fort, a personalized sanctuary to use as an escape from the boogeyman. All that was missing was a tin can telephone line or a walkie-talkie allowing him to find a friendly voice in the dark.

Digging his cell phone out of his pocket, he stared at it, debating whether to succumb to instinct. The timing was bad. He'd just been with Ben, after all. What was he doing? What was he thinking?

"Ah, fuck it," he sighed. Maybe his willpower had been beaten down by the scene or his orgasm. The decadence had left him wanting more of anything that would make him feel good.

The number was saved, and was one of those he dialed most. It took just two taps of his fingers and the line was ringing. He felt like an ass and rubbed his face, staring at those pills, wondering if he should hang up before the call was answered.

It rang two and a half times.

"Kyle?"

"Hey. 'Sup?"

"Nothing, man. How are you? I was just getting back from work, actually."

Darrek's voice made Kyle smile hugely, as it always did. The sound of it in his ear was the very definition of warm and fuzzy. It was kind of sad, really. He was like a schoolgirl talking to her biggest crush. He even started to draw spirals on the bedspread with his fingertip, like he was tracing all of the things he should be saying but wouldn't.

"Yeah, well, if you lived up here, we could hang out… watch the game… order some tacos…"

Darrek laughed heartily and Kyle's grin grew so wide, his cheeks hurt.

"Wow, tacos would be amazing right now, actually," Darrek murmured. "Are you reading my mind?"

"Yep. I have superpowers now. That's what happens when you move out of Mommy and Daddy's house. Magical things, Dare. Magical."

"God, I miss you."

Kyle grabbed the immaculately arranged baggie, crumpling it in his fist and pressed it against his forehead. He made the effort to force his voice to sound normal, not thick and teary like it felt, and answered, "Yeah, I don't miss you at all."

"Liar. You called *me*, you know."

The fucking tears started to fall anyway and he let the pause draw out too long. He had to. If he said anything, Darrek would have been able to hear it in his voice and that would have been so much worse than making him wonder.

"Hey, you all right?" Darrek added when Kyle said nothing.

"I'm such a *liar*," Kyle sighed, then laughed, wiping his eyes dry.

"It's not like that's a new development, dude. Don't let it get you down," Darrek said easily, though Kyle could hear it in his tone that he was playing along for Kyle's benefit, but was reading between the lines like only a best friend could.

Kyle asked, "What're you up to, anyway? What have I missed?"

Darrek sighed into the phone. Kyle could hear him moving around. A door shut. Keys jingled. He imagined Darrek's house and Darrek going inside. It came alive in Kyle's memory, so vivid it was like he was already high and hallucinating. He wished he could ask if anyone else was home, if Darrek was coming home to an empty house like Kyle had, or not. There was no normal way to ask, so he let it go, and just listened for other voices.

"Oh, you know," Darrek told him, helpfully bypassing the fact that Kyle had just gotten choked up. Darrek was a good guy. He knew how to make you feel comfortable. "Going out with Sara once I get washed up. There's a new bistro downtown that she wants to try, but there's a bunch of stores down there too. I think it's just an excuse to shop and ask me to pay for it all." He laughed it off.

Kyle shook his head. "Dude, you are *whipped*. Is that why you can't afford to move out? You're spending your whole paycheck on *Sara*?"

"Hey, she's worth it. Plus, you're one to talk. I know you shell out a fair share on all of those girlfriends of yours. How many is it now? Last time I asked, it was down to four."

The conversation caused him to think of Ben, and the money he'd agreed to pay as Ben's fee. It would be a regular expense, but well worth the gains. "Oh, you know. I get around. It's not like I'm buying anyone diamonds or anything. Look, I'll let you go. Call me sometime, okay? There aren't a hell of a lot of people I can talk to up here."

"Will do. Take care, ya hear?"

"You too. Later, Dare."

They hung up. Kyle dropped the phone and the crumpled baggie. For a while he just stared at nothing, feeling strange and lost.

Kyle didn't know what Ben saw when he looked Kyle's way. Imagination didn't provide any answers, either. There was no distancing what Kyle felt in order to be able to conjure a clearer picture of who he actually presented to the world, sans personal details Kyle never intended to reveal. Did Ben like his darkness, or did he ignore all evidence in favor of physical attraction? Typically, Kyle's partners were of the ignoring type. The search was still on for someone who could handle who Kyle truly was.

There was a lot to like about Ben. He wasn't afraid to touch, for one, or to own his desire. Sure, Ben liked his rules. As a professional Dom, how could he not? But he was willing to let Kyle set some rules of his own, too. That difference helped things feel controlled, and safer than they might otherwise. Some of the wildness Kyle needed to hide in public, from his co-workers, peers, or even people like Darrek, Kyle could unleash with Ben. It was all in that paperwork. Bloodplay was fine. Breathplay was fine. Ben could pierce Kyle's skin, whip him, or try to scare the shit out of him. It didn't matter. What Kyle had already lived through would always be worse. Part of Kyle even wanted to try to find something worse, just to cancel out the bad memories.

So, Ben was a possibility.

The urge to get stoned was less strong than usual. The desire to cut himself was almost nonexistent.

He wound up sticking the baggie back in the drawer, untouched, and sincerely hoped Darrek had a good time that night with Sara. He deserved some happiness, more than anyone else Kyle knew.

A month passed and Ben's schedule filled up with regulars and new-comers alike. At the end of one sunny Saturday at Diadem, between appointments with an old favorite—Dmitri—and Kyle, Ben walked Dmitri to his motorcycle. He kept an eye on how Dmitri moved, his breathing and the level of tiredness he displayed through subtle cues like the position of his shoulders. It'd been a hell of a scene, full of edging, breathplay, and finished off spectacularly with Ben coming so hard inside the glorious sheath of Dmitri's ass, he saw stars.

Outside of Diadem, Ben pulled Dmitri against him by the lapels of his motorcycle jacket, loving the way Dmitri's dark, Italian coloring looked next to all of that black leather. They kissed until Ben's hand began to creep back up to Dmitri's throat, where he was sure bruises were already rising to the surface. Pushing away from the kiss before he was drawn in further, Ben couldn't look away from his slave's lips as Dmitri murmured in a gruff rasp, "Thank you, Master."

"Mm, no, thank *you*." Ben sucked the taste of him from his lower lip and watched Dmitri climb onto his bike. "Drive safely. Send me a text once you're home."

"Absolutely," Dmitri grinned. "I'm looking forward to Wednes-day."

"Oh, me too," Ben chuckled, smiling helplessly, "Believe me. Take care of yourself until then."

The bike roared to life. Dmitri took it easy on his way out of the lot and down the long drive to the main road. Ben was glad to see it. He didn't want his slave taking any chances that could get him hurt.

As he began to realize he should get back inside and start prep for Kyle, Ben heard from directly behind him, in sharp question, "Who was that?"

Ben spun around.

"You're here early," were the first words out of his mouth.

Kyle stood there, arms folded, seething. He was so mad, Ben was surprised there wasn't actual steam coming out of his young, beauti-ful slave's ears.

"I couldn't wait. Wanted to see you. And then I see you tonguing *that* asshole," Kyle snapped.

"Whoa. Whoa." Ben held up his hands and shook his head with amazement. "Are you out of your fucking *mind*, slave?"

Crossing the space between them rapidly, Ben grabbed Kyle's arm, pushing the sleeve up before checking the other. Then he took hold of Kyle's chin and carefully pulled his eyelids farther open with his fingertips. Kyle bore it with a scowl.

As soon as Ben failed to find signs of drug use, he ordered, "Get the fuck inside. Now."

Kyle yelled, "Not until you tell me who that was!"

Ben grabbed Kyle by the shoulder, pushed him down to his knees and planted a boot on his shoulder to keep him down.

"*That* was my obedient, well-behaved slave of... let's see... five years? Control the fucking attitude. Now."

Kyle glared up at him, full of piss and spit, ready to fight and rage. It was going to be a heck of scene, Ben could taste it.

"I'm a fucking Dominant for hire. *You* are my paying submissive client. Get your shit together. The world does not revolve around you. Surely you know this."

Ben could see that there was an argument playing out inside Kyle's head. This wasn't about Dmitri. Not precisely, anyway. Kyle would never let on what he was really angry about if he could help it, though. It wasn't his style. Kyle liked to keep everything under a lid and only let out the things he chose very selectively and with proper forethought. Sure, he'd get extremely pissed off, but he wouldn't be honest about why or say what was really on his mind. Not in a million years. After only a few weeks, Ben already knew his new client at least that well.

So, Ben took a guess.

"I know what this is," Ben grinned. "You thought you were my favorite, right?"

It struck a nerve. Kyle went from enraged to on the verge of tears in the blink of an eye.

He pushed at Ben's leg to get the boot off of his shoulder. "Get the fuck off of me. I'm going home," Kyle growled miserably.

"Wow. You're really that much of a child?" Ben scoffed, making sure Kyle couldn't budge his leg an inch, even if it meant Kyle got a scrape on his shoulder from the boot. He didn't intend for Kyle to be able to get up or go anywhere Ben didn't want him to go. "Gonna take your toys and go home to play by yourself? Where's the fun in that?"

Eyes averted, Kyle stopped fighting, became still. That's when Ben knew he had him.

"Cool off, come inside. We'll talk about video possibilities. You're still interested, right? Extra cash. Extra playtime. Fame and fans galore."

Kyle softened even more, but not all the way. Not yet.

"You have any other clients coming after me tonight?" Kyle asked, with only a smidgeon of bitterness.

"Nope. You're it, kiddo."

"Good."

"Good? Is this more jealousy?"

"Not exactly," Kyle answered, a flash of a devious grin twisting up the side of his mouth. It was the sort of look that made Ben really look forward to getting Kyle naked and bound, so he could wipe that smirk off his face in the most creative ways possible. "I want to revise my contract, before we start."

"What the hell are you up to?" Ben asked in a low growl, squinting down at Kyle's 'up-to-something' face.

A few minutes later, he found out. Ben stood on one side of the desk in Diadem's office while Kyle stood on the other, bent over a new contract which he was diligently filling out. The only notable difference—and it was quite fucking notable—was that Kyle was suddenly okay with pegging and penetration, though still not sex.

Without anything resembling a witty comeback, Ben stroked his short beard and considered what this implied for the coming evening.

Soon, Kyle was finished with the contract. They both signed, and Gabriel—who was there to assist Ben that evening with dominating duties—added a third witness signature to make it all nice and official. Gabriel was glancing curiously between Ben's thoughtful squint and Kyle's troublemaker grin. After a moment in which they both waited for him to say something, Ben said to Kyle in surrender, "Okay, you win."

"Awesome, I love when I win," Kyle said happily.

Chapter 5

Two on One

It was a momentous evening for Ben Knox. A leather hood masked half of his face. Gabriel was wearing an identical one. Ben stood in the dungeon of Diadem, watching Kyle. Ben and Gabriel were also both bare-chested, wearing black pants and boots. The similarity was intentional. Maybe it would help ease Kyle into being comfortable with Gabriel's presence during a scene, as an acting Dom. They had only included Gabriel as an assisting Dom twice before, and in a very limited role. Slowly, Ben was including Gabriel more and more. This time, he intended to let Gabriel do most of the work, while ensuring Kyle knew it was Ben who was solely in charge of what was happening to him.

Kyle's favoritism toward Ben was understandable, especially given the prolonged interview process he chose to go through, but if Kyle consented to having multiple Doms in charge of him — which he had — it forced him to stop thinking so much about who, specifically, was interacting with him, and react on a more basic level of slave to Master. That meant if Kyle saw one of his Masters near him, that was all that mattered, not *which* Master. His obedience should be the same, whether it was Ben he was faced with, or Gabriel.

There were some visible differences between the Doms, though. Ben's neatly trimmed beard was a giveaway, given Gabriel's cleanly shaved jaw, as was Ben's more plentiful chest hair.

Kyle was still wearing his pants, though he'd left his shoes and shirt by the far wall. He seemed perplexed by Ben's order that he not remove all of his clothes, and the implications behind why Ben might not have wanted him naked just yet. There was a sweet little frown line, right between Kyle's blond eyebrows. His stance was wide, his hands held stiffly behind his back. Ben, with his arms folded under his pecs, circled slowly around Kyle, taking in the details, wondering still about the change in contract details.

The real question was how hard to push and where the newly redrawn lines were, exactly. Just because Kyle wanted to experiment with penetration didn't mean the issues originally making penetration a problem were miraculously gone. They were still there, just buried or shifted around a little. Ben and Gabriel would need to remain mindful of that. The last thing Ben wanted was to betray a slave's fragile trust as soon as he showed signs of really opening up.

Maybe that little frown line wasn't about the clothing at all.

"How are you feeling, slave?"

Ben walked his circle. Gabriel was preparing the equipment, glancing their way occasionally, watching them as Ben watched Kyle, just like he'd done up in the office over the paperwork. They were all trying to figure each other out. It was all one big mind-fuck.

"Good, Sir. Thank you, Sir."

"Is that bullshit?"

Hesitation. "No, Sir."

"Nervous?"

"No, Sir."

That was interesting, because he truthfully *didn't* look nervous. It was something else that was irking Goldilocks, something harder to pin down. And that was worse than nervousness.

Maybe it was drugs.

"Jonesing?"

Kyle's gaze darted away from Ben as he came strolling around in his circle again, and they were suddenly face-to-face.

"Don't fucking lie to me, slave."

"Yes, Sir. Sorry, Sir."

"So, you're fighting the urge to use. Is that all?"

More hesitation. "I don't know, Sir."

The bitch of it was that of all things, Kyle looked *sad*. If there was any label for the particular expression on his adorable, sexy, deceptively angelic face, it was that, and of all possible emotions to be experiencing at that precise moment, sadness was the one which made

Ben's job the hardest to accomplish. Kyle was in a place which was at the opposite end of the spectrum from where Ben wanted him.

Standing in Kyle's personal space, it was all-too-easy to see the tension build in Kyle's form, the diligent avoidance of eye contact, and the tiredness reflected in his expression. Kyle was clenching his jaw and gritting his teeth, but almost leaning in to Ben rather than shrinking from him. Experimentally, Ben shifted fractionally forward and the pace of Kyle's breathing seemed to slow subtly.

"Have you been obeying my orders, slave?" Ben asked firmly, but quietly.

"Yes, Sir."

"Look at me."

Kyle's gaze rose in increments, until his summer-sky-on-a-clear-day blue eyes were steadily trained on Ben's face. A muscle in Kyle's jaw twitched. His lips were pressed tightly together.

Ben let the moment draw out. The tension in Kyle didn't lessen. It didn't grow either.

"What do you need?"

"Submission," Kyle answered in a breath of sound between gritted teeth, too quiet, probably, for Gabriel to hear. His wickedly intelligent gaze darted back and forth between Ben's eyes.

Needing to submit was part of it, but there was more. Since Kyle would never admit to the rest, it was up to Ben to figure it out on his own. He decided to do a little trial and error to see if he could hone in on the truth tucked meticulously out of reach behind Kyle's walls.

"Hunter!" Ben called without looking around. "Gimme a hand with this."

Bingo. Right away, in nothing more than the rapid, precise shift of Kyle's gaze to where Gabriel stood, and a subtle tightness around Kyle's mouth, Ben was able to guess Gabriel was setting off some of Kyle's alarms.

The question, though, was why.

They'd all been here together. Was it the combined force of the contract changes *and* Gabriel's presence pushing Kyle's stress button?

Ben backed off, pacing a little, staying alert. Gabriel's boots connected solidly with the concrete floor as he walked over. Circling around Kyle, Gabriel came up behind him. Gabriel's focus was on Kyle, but Ben knew he was just waiting for direction from Ben.

The closer Gabriel came, the more Kyle's tension notched up. His breathing quickened. His gaze was locked on to Ben, as if in a plea. But, a plea for what? Mercy? Was Kyle regretting the last minute relaxation of his self-imposed rules?

"Secure his wrists first."

Gabriel stepped up close to Kyle's back, taking hold of his wrists, pinning them together and drawing them upward to limit Kyle's range of motion. His muscles flexed as Gabriel forced Kyle's arms further upward. Kyle's chin tipped upward slightly, but his gaze was still locked to Ben. His nostrils flared with each indrawn breath. There was anger there, beneath the surface. Interesting.

"Good," Ben smiled. "Now, give him a hand."

That little frown line in Kyle's brow deepened momentarily, the sentiment behind it echoing in a brief downward tilt of the corners of his lips as Gabriel reached around Kyle's waist, popped the button of his fly, and slipped a gloved hand inside Kyle's pants, all while maintaining the hold on his wrists.

Just by watching Kyle's expression, Ben could tell what Gabriel was doing to him. A heavy exhale wasn't immediately followed by an inhale as Kyle temporarily stopped breathing. This indicated that Gabriel had taken hold of Kyle's cock. When Kyle's lips unsealed themselves, parting ever-so-slightly around that delayed inhale, followed by a mostly undetectable shiver, it meant Gabriel's grip was sliding along Kyle's shaft.

Then, Kyle closed his eyes.

"Eyes on me," Ben ordered immediately, pointing to his own eyes with his index and middle fingers.

Kyle's eyes opened, but his gaze remained unfocused, even if it was pointed in Ben's general direction. He wasn't seeing Ben at all. He was somewhere else; maybe pretending it wasn't Gabriel touching his dick.

"Hunter, punishment," Ben said sharply. Kyle's focus sharpened instantly, the look he gave Ben laced with mild panic.

"No—" Kyle started, but the word became lost in a shout. His form sagged as his knees momentarily buckled before he caught himself and masked his expression. Gabriel yanked Kyle's pinned wrists upward, forcing him to straighten completely. Kyle's shout cut off before the pain did. Ben let the moment breathe, sharing a look with Gabriel, who was calm and collected, his fist squeezing Kyle's testicles.

Kyle's breathing grew erratic, peppered with low growls. He started to sweat, to tremble, and seemed annoyed his discomfort was evident. That annoyance bothered Ben. He wanted Kyle reacting honestly, not manipulating his reactions according to what he thought his Masters wanted to see.

"Harder," Ben told Gabriel.

Kyle's eyebrows rose in unspoken supplication right as Gabriel acted. His remaining composure breaking, Kyle panted, then yelled, "Stop! Fuck!"

Ben lifted a hand, all fingers curled in except for his index and middle fingers, which extended upward. Twisting them in the air, he communicated his direction clearly to his assistant. The muscles of Gabriel's arm flexed as his grip shifted. Kyle made a frantic sound on his next exhale, fighting Gabriel's hold on his wrists, and his hold on Kyle's balls. The pitch of Kyle's cry rose.

"Are you ready to obey my simple, direct orders, slave?" Ben asked. "When I say 'eyes on me', it means look at me. It means *focus*. It doesn't mean pretend to look at me while you daydream about god knows what. I see you drift again like that, we'll have a problem. Problems equal punishment and each punishment will be worse — and more creative — than the last."

At first Kyle's mouth moved soundlessly, his expression still pleading, the pain making it more of a challenge to find breath to speak. Ben twisted his upraised fingers the other way and Kyle yelled a moment later as Gabriel sharply twisted his handful of flesh in a similar direction.

"Yes, Sir!" Kyle managed roughly. "Sorry, Sir!"

Ben splayed his fingers. Gabriel loosened his grip. Kyle gasped for air. His gaze was focused and alert, though. He looked right into Ben's eyes, showing him he was paying attention and not getting lost in his head. Whatever was in there, haunting Kyle, was no good. Ben didn't want him going there, he wanted Kyle invested in the present moment.

"Continue," Ben murmured to Gabriel.

Kyle groaned in protest, likely too sore to entirely enjoy being fondled.

"You just keep looking right at me like that, slave," Ben told Kyle as he writhed a little in discomfort, like he was trying not to, but couldn't help it. Maybe he'd do well with more restraints. Ben made a mental note.

Gabriel's hand was moving, kneading inside Kyle's opened pants—low in the crotch. Playing with Kyle's balls would give him no relief, only different types of torment, which was just as Ben intended. He didn't want Kyle getting off, he wanted Kyle to *feel*.

"You want him to stop that?" Ben asked Kyle. "Hmm?"

"Yes," Kyle grumbled through his teeth, adding as an after-thought, "Sir."

"Tough shit," Ben replied. "Hunter, keep him on his toes."

Minutes passed. Ben and Kyle watched only each other. It seemed to take all of Kyle's effort to endure Gabriel's touch. Sometimes he hissed sharply, sometimes he shuddered, or panted. Gabriel knew to mix pain into the pleasure, to toy with Kyle's balls until he was desperate for a reprieve, willing to do anything to make it stop. It was fun as hell for Ben to get to enjoy the show.

"This slave's dick is leaking on my wrist," Gabriel said after a while. Kyle's breathing was shallow and he was drawn up on his toes.

"Sore?" Ben asked Kyle, who nodded in reply. "No, tell me. *Speak.*"

First he grunted, his eyes rolling back. Quickly, he caught himself, drew his gaze back to Ben and said, "Yes, Sir."

"What's it gonna be, slave?" Ben asked, stepping closer. "Pain or pleasure? Or pleasure *through* pain?"

Something brightened behind Kyle's steady gaze, igniting like a spark burning hot, but cooling fast once thrown from the fire.

Gotcha, Ben thought. Kyle was getting off on the pain. He wanted more of it, so Ben intended to give him something different, instead.

"Stroke his dick. Gently," Ben said to Gabriel, smiling at Kyle.

Kyle attempted to hide his displeasure at this bait and switch tactic, but failed miserably. As Gabriel's hand began to pump Kyle's cock, Kyle's frown grew more and more anguished, his lips slightly more parted, his breathing growing even quicker. It would have been easier for him if he'd been allowed to close his eyes, but that was the whole point. Kyle needed to know he was seen and who was — and was *not* — touching him. If pain was a safe place for him, Ben would push him the other way in order to test his boundaries.

When Kyle made a soft groan and his eyes rolled again, very slightly, Ben felt it as a shiver of excitement, racing under his skin, giving him goosebumps as he tried to imagine exactly how hard Kyle was in that moment. Ben knew from personal experience how good Gabriel was at stroking cock. When anal was off the table, as it was with Gabriel, other skills became magnified and specialized.

The whole picture came alive for Ben. Kyle wanted to hurt, and to fight the hurt. That must have been what he'd been relying on before he came to Diadem. The drugs and self-harm indicated as much. Pleasure, care, scrutiny, examination, and patience were things Kyle ran from. Those were the tools he was giving Ben to use to take him apart.

It went on like that for a while, with Gabriel's tenderness slowly dismantling Kyle's defenses. From the edge of his vision, Ben saw Gabriel's arm pumping as he tugged steadily, but kept staring right into Kyle's eyes. Soon, Kyle's frown was gone entirely. Mouth relaxed, eyes half-lidded, Kyle's fight turned a corner. Then, he was fighting something entirely different than what he had been initially.

Still, Ben didn't put a stop to it, and as Kyle's need to push against the hand working him closer and closer to a climax grew, he began to shudder slightly. Every breath came with a soft moan.

"Don't come," Ben teased in a sing-song voice. Kyle's eyes were fixed hard on him, like maybe just by looking at Ben, Kyle could make it all stop. The sensations and stimulation from Gabriel were destroying Kyle's ability to fight back. He grew weaker. Ben could practically see the cracks forming in Kyle's cherished fortifications. His moans merged together, became a low sort of purr.

That was it. That was what Ben had been waiting for.

"Stop," Ben said to Gabriel, finally. "Show me."

Gabriel's pumping ceased. He withdrew his hand and pushed the fabric of Kyle's pants gently out of the way, exposing his incredibly stiff, reddened cock, shiny wet with plenty of pre-come slicking the shaft and glistening around the head. Ben lowered his gaze to it, appreciating Gabriel's work. Being thus displayed caused Kyle's erection to twitch in appreciation.

Slowly, Ben unfolded his arms and reached out with a single hand, brushing the underside of Kyle's cockhead with the back of a knuckle, barely grazing the skin. A harder moan erupted from Kyle from the contact with his true Master. Immediately, he fought to get it together, but it was too late. Ben savored the triumph of seeing Kyle's raw, pure need displayed so brazenly. His mask had slipped off. He'd allowed himself to be vulnerable.

"Slave," Ben started, speaking unhurriedly. "I want you to lace your fingers behind your head and stay perfectly still."

Humming as he fought noticeably for control, Kyle lowered his arms, now released from Gabriel's grip, then raised them, bringing both up behind his head, as directed. Chest rising and falling steadily, arms flexing again as he settled into the position, Kyle lowered his chin slightly but kept his gaze trained on his Master. His hair was plastered to his forehead with sweat and small tremors wracked him. In all of their time together thus far, Ben had never seen Kyle in such an open, wild state. Though Kyle obviously knew how exposed he was in that moment, literally and figuratively, he seemed to understand there was no way to hide. It was too late. Ben had seen too much and there was no tucking anything back into the dark.

Kyle hated being displayed, but, at the same time, he seemed to *need* it. While made as vulnerable as he'd ever been, with just a look, Kyle dared Ben to make a wrong move. The safeword was right on the tip of his tongue. He wanted Ben to give him a reason to use it. It was the only valid way out of there and back to where he was safe with his lies and pain. Any other escape route would mean sacrificing pride and there was no way Kyle would do that. Everything in Kyle screamed for Ben to fuck up. One wrong move and it would be over for good.

So, Ben edged carefully over Kyle's line drawn in the sand with a nod to Gabriel.

Gabriel shifted Kyle's pants a little lower, pushing them as far as they'd comfortably go with his legs spread as they were. Then, Gabriel caressed up the back of Kyle's thigh to the curve of his ass.

As soon as Kyle fidgeted, Ben repeated, "*Perfectly* still, slave."

He moved back into Kyle's personal space and, once again, lightly caressed the underside of Kyle's cockhead, lest his erection wilt under the barrage of fear. There was no way to be certain of the precise moment when Gabriel's touch ventured into the crease of Kyle's ass, parting his cheeks, but Ben had no doubt of when Kyle was breached by Gabriel's lubricated fingertip.

Whimpering sharply, Kyle closed his eyes with a heavy frown. Ben softened his voice and took hold of Kyle's jaw with his left hand, saying, "Breathe in through your nose. Hold it. Now blow it out."

A louder cry told Ben the finger had moved deeper, but Kyle was breathing more deeply, as ordered. Rubbing a little harder with the back of his finger, feeling Kyle's flesh push into the contact, chasing it, Ben told him, "That's your Master's touch you feel, slave. Your Master takes care of you. He protects you. That's a reward, not a punishment. You want him inside you as much as you want to come."

"Yes, Master," Kyle murmured.

"Ready to submit to us, slave?" Ben asked softly.

"Fuck yes," Kyle replied. It was half grimace, half groan.

"How's that feel?"

Kyle's mouth fell open. Another cry wrenched free as his lower lip quivered. That meant Gabriel's finger was moving.

"Fuckin' *tight*," Gabriel answered.

Ben wrapped Kyle's dick with his whole hand and squeezed along the shaft, then tugged.

"No... fuck..." Kyle hissed, trembling bodily and thrusting shallowly, helplessly, against Ben's grip. Swiping a thumb over Kyle's tip, Ben watched as he melted into the bombardment of sensation. The hiss became a moan.

"Better," Gabriel said.

"He's taking it?"

"Yep."

Ben leaned in until his lips were near the shell of Kyle's ear and whispered, "Love when you get wet for me."

Kyle's head tipped to the side, exposing more of his neck to Ben. He thrust harder against Ben's hand, riding it.

"*Much* better," Gabriel said with a smile.

Chapter 6
Exposed

They got Kyle onto one of the padded leather tables and set his feet in stirrups. Ben could feel Kyle submitting, even if there was still some reluctance in him, waiting for everything to go south in a bad way. Ben added trust issues to the mental tally he was keeping on Kyle, though his selectiveness when Dom shopping gave that away a long time ago.

It was important to keep Kyle's face in view in order to better judge his mood and reactions. Ben wanted to know instantly if something they were doing was triggering Kyle. He wanted to know before *Kyle* even knew. The whole point was to keep him invested, keep him enjoying the scene. Where they were with Kyle was a step in the process, not an end goal.

So, Kyle was able to let Gabriel finger-fuck him. Great. That wasn't nearly enough for Ben, not when he sensed how much more Kyle was capable of giving.

Kyle was told to undress completely before getting onto the table. There was an overhead light shining down on him, putting him on display. He seemed to relax more once his feet were strapped into the stirrups, so Ben added additional restraints. Kyle's arms were held in leather cuffs affixed to the table by his sides. His head was cradled, for the time being, on a headrest at the top of the table, which could be lowered or released. While Ben fit a metal dental gag in Kyle's mouth, forcing his jaws open wide and keeping his tongue held down, Gabriel lubed up his fingers and stayed near the lower end of the table. First, he slipped a vibrating ring around Kyle's dick, shifting it to hug just under the head, and switched it on. Kyle groaned and closed his eyes.

Gabriel gently kneaded Kyle's scrotum, then rubbed over the patch of skin just behind it. Without hesitation, he slid his index finger up Kyle's ass.

Kyle cried out, but the gag made speaking impossible. It was only sound. Kyle's safe sign was to snap his fingers, so Ben was glad to see his hands relaxed inside the bonds. The rest of his body was far from relaxed, though. Anxiousness sang from every inch of him.

Releasing the headrest, Ben eased Kyle's head back until his throat was in a nice, straight line, his mouth open and ready.

Freeing himself from his pants, Ben rolled on a condom and heard Kyle moan heavily.

"Want it?" Ben teased.

Kyle moaned again, in answer. When Ben entered Kyle's mouth, his cock sliding effortlessly into Kyle's throat, he moaned, too. Caressing the side of Kyle's neck as he thrust in and pulled back out, Ben watched Gabriel's finger work, pumping into Kyle's ass every time Ben pushed into his mouth.

Gabriel glanced at Ben, asking without saying a word.

"Do it," Ben rasped, riding the hot, wet glove of Kyle's throat.

Reaching for Kyle's dick, Gabriel took hold of it, then began stroking. A second finger slipped in beside the first and Kyle quivered violently. His hips snapped up against Gabriel's hand on his cock, fucking it. The fingers up Kyle's ass went in to the hilt, stuffing it full and Kyle moaned loudly. Then he was coming, shuddering as he pushed and pushed and *pushed* against Gabriel's fist while semen flowed white over Gabriel's gloved fingers. Gabriel used it as lube and stroked him through it while the fingers pumped inside Kyle's ass.

Ben pulled out without coming. When he released the dental gag, Kyle was staring right at Ben's erection.

"Please let me," Kyle begged hoarsely. He whimpered softly as Gabriel's fingers again thrust inward.

But Ben just tucked himself away, and shifted the headrest back into position, smiling at Kyle's expression of profound, bratty disappointment, which washed away most of the fear provoked by being violated by Gabriel. Each small victory only spurred Ben on.

Gabriel removed the vibrating ring and wiped Kyle down. They gave him a moment to recover before continuing.

Quietly, without commentary, Kyle tracked them both as Gabriel went to the supply tray and Ben walked down to the lower end of the table, trailing a hand down along Kyle's thigh as he went. As soon as Ben pulled a pair of latex gloves from the box, Kyle yanked at the arm restraints, as if to remind himself they were there. Once Ben had the gloves on, Kyle closed his eyes.

"You want this easy or spicy?" Ben asked.

At first, there was no answer. With the tips of the fingers of both of his hands, Ben pulled at Kyle's cheeks, spreading him open. His hole was rubbed pink and slippery wet with lube. He clenched up upon inspection and Ben just pulled harder, getting his fingers closer to that pink knot and prying at it.

"Answer. Now."

Kyle whimpered. "Spicy," he managed, his voice breaking and breathy.

Ben gave Gabriel a nod.

"Okay. Distraction it is. You're not afraid of a little pain, are you, slave?"

"No, Sir," Kyle responded, sounding steadier, but panting.

"Good. So, while I'm stuffing *this* little pink hole, Master Gabe is going to be stuffing another one. How's that *sound*?"

"Funny," Kyle groaned, eyeing the long, slender urethral sound in Gabriel's hand. He slicked it with lube while Kyle winced with dread.

"Nervous?" Ben grinned, running the pad of his thumb along the edge of Kyle's rim. "Good. Hold on to that."

Staring at Gabriel's hands preparing the sound, Kyle then tracked Gabriel as he brought it, one-handed to the table and took hold of Kyle's flaccid penis.

"Do it," Kyle growled. "Finger me."

"You want me to?" Ben asked, surprised.

Gabriel lined up the blunt, narrow tip of the sound with the small opening of Kyle's urethra, after swiping more lube over it. He touched the metal to flesh and Kyle shuddered hard, blowing out air through his mouth. "God. Fuck. Hell. God, *I hate it*. Fuck!"

The sound had begun to drop, ever-so-slowly into him, parting his slit. Kyle let out a primal, ear-splitting cry of pain and fight. His hands balled into fists and he closed his eyes, trying to breathe through it. But, the deeper the metal sound went, stuffing his dark, wet cock, the redder Kyle's face got and the wilder his shouts. He was clearly in a lot of pain. Gabriel lightly stroked Kyle's shaft all the while. Ben played with Kyle's balls with one hand and rubbed back and forth over his asshole with the other. By the time the sound was halfway inside, Kyle was semi-erect and had stopped clenching up. When it was fully inserted, there were tears slipping silently down the sides of his face, but his mouth was relaxed and his eyes opened.

"Easy," Ben hushed, slipping two fingers through Kyle's rim. The muscle of his sphincter hugged them tightly. It felt soft and snug, hot and perfect. Kyle clenched and tilted his hips slightly as the fingers slid into him, then moaned as Ben spread his fingers apart, prying him open and sheathing himself in the soft, gripping passage. Kyle let out a soft little mewl and tipped his head back slightly in the headrest, gazing at the ceiling rather than the man who was playing in his ass. Ben built a rhythm, moving into Kyle's body, pulling slightly back out, only to do it again and again.

There was no fight left in him. The reluctance was gone. Kyle was purely in a submissive mindset. No conditions. No walls. Just trust. Kyle let Ben push, take and explore. Amazed, Ben watched, enraptured, as Kyle gave himself over to it. His cock was stuffed with the sound. Silver gleamed within the pink, tender flesh. Ben massaged Kyle's balls, tugging on them when they drew up. Slipping his fingers out completely, Ben gazed at the loosened ring of muscle, then stuffed it full again with three rather than two.

Kyle sighed and allowed it, clenching in flutters around Ben's fingers. He had his eyes closed. Ben closed his as well, imagining it wasn't just his fingers entering Kyle, riding out the virginal tightness of him and provoking those sweet little sounds.

"Does it hurt?" Ben asked.

"Not enough," Kyle moaned, peering down at him.

He gave Kyle's balls a hard yank and Kyle's eyes rolled up in his head, his hips chasing up off the table. Ben yanked again, squeezing as well, as hard as he dared, and Kyle sobbed, his cock an angry red, swollen thick around the sound.

"Take it out," he told Gabriel. "Get me a condom."

As soon as the instrument was free of him, Ben rolled the condom onto Kyle and swallowed him down a moment later, without hesitation or pride. Ben moaned, sucking hard on him, loving the feel of Kyle's cock filling his mouth. Kyle bucked, undulating up against Ben's mouth as Ben fingered Kyle's ass with most of his hand. With a hard gasp, Kyle came a second time, then purred on the way down, rocking gently through the aftershocks.

The water ran hot in the shower, steaming up the room. Gabriel was cleaning up the dungeon. Ben lingered inside the shower room, watching Kyle stand with his head bowed, hands braced against the white tile wall under the spray in one of the stalls. Low walls separated them, but there was little privacy to be found there. Privacy was beside the point. Overhead lights were strung in lines down the center of the long room. They cast shadows and shone a slightly yellowish fluorescent light which reflected from the gleaming walls and floor. It was bright in there, almost too much. There was no hiding anything. The center of it all was the gorgeous young man, still flushed from two orgasms, lingering in the room's last stall—the farthest from the door.

Almost shyly, Kyle called out, "Ben?"

"Yeah," Ben replied, walking down to where Kyle waited.

When he got to Kyle's stall, Kyle gave him a long look, up and down Ben's body, from over his shoulder. Then, he turned away again, letting the water spray his face and the side of his neck, then blew out a fine mist of droplets as he bowed his head again.

"Join me," Kyle said, quietly. "Please."

Ben debated it. He really did, even more than he would have thought possible. He couldn't even put his finger on *why* he was debating it.

But there was no saying no, as much as instinct told him to. And fuck if instinct wasn't shrieking its head off at his libido.

Ben stripped down and stepped, naked, into the stall.

Kyle kept his back turned but spread his legs more, arching his back a little more, too, so that his ass looked amazing, like he was trying to focus Ben's attention on it. Ben moved up behind him, getting wet, kissing the side of Kyle's neck and circling an arm around to palm Kyle's abdomen. Water ran hot over them both, skin against skin. Their breathing seemed overloud in the echo-filled chamber. Sweating and slipping against each other, movement was easy and fluid.

Kyle reached back, finding Ben's bare cock. He stroked the shaft, moaning softly as the column slid slickly in his grip.

When Kyle shifted its angle, lining Ben's erection up with his opening, Ben was the one trembling. He clasped Kyle's hip, his fingers denting the skin. Frowning against what he felt happening, and what it felt like he was doing to that strangely broken young man, Ben pleaded in an unheeded whisper, "Don't..."

But it was too late, Kyle pressed back onto him, his inner muscles pulling Ben in. A second later, they were joined and Ben heard the faint sound of Kyle's weeping before he was able to master himself and push the sadness down again.

"Damn it, Kyle," Ben cursed, quietly enough that he didn't think Kyle heard him.

The worst part was that he didn't stop—*couldn't* stop. He began to move because Kyle's lithe body was so hot and tight, gripping him. Sheathed completely, soon Ben was panting, caressing Kyle everywhere. He caught Kyle's chin and kissed him from over his shoulder while thrusting carefully. When their eyes locked, the sadness was gone like it had never been there at all. Ben thrust harder, snapping his hips as need overtook reason. Kyle moaned, taking it without complaint. He planted his hands on the wall and let Ben move within him while rolling his hips slightly, perfectly, counter to every push.

Ben pulled out without coming, growling and fighting the huge swell of pleasure threatening to wash over him and wipe it all away. When he opened his eyes, Kyle had turned around, toward him and he was leaning in. They kissed, and Kyle's tongue was suddenly in Ben's mouth, just as Kyle's hand moved in the spraying water, washing off Ben's hot, straining cock.

Kyle sank to his knees, the kiss broken. Stunned silent, Ben stared down at Kyle as he steadied Ben's erection, then moved to suckle the tip, stroking the rest with a hand which twisted up and down the shaft.

Ben caught a flicker of dark movement out of the corner of his eye, and glanced to his right, down the long line of stalls. Gabriel stood in the doorway, watching them with quite evident disapproval. Then he turned and left, right before Ben shouted roughly with the onslaught of his orgasm. Cradling Kyle's head in both hands, Ben came in a flood over his tongue. Lips kissed around Ben's thickness, Kyle hummed and stroked and had the most peaceful look on his face. When Ben was fully spent, Kyle, sitting on his heels, tenderly kissed the inside of Ben's hip and the top of his thigh, embracing him almost reverently. With a hitching sigh and eyes slightly red from crying, Kyle rested his cheek against Ben's left thigh and held him. If there were more tears, the water washed them right away.

That's when Ben knew. That was the precise moment.

What had happened in that shower wasn't a matter of Master and slave, or even just the actions of a young man acting out of pain or loneliness. It was purely a human being in need, taking a chance and reaching out to connect with someone he felt might be able to understand.

And Ben understood, as he had when he walked into Trace's living room, years ago, and saw an eerily lovely, haunted, dark-haired teenager named after an angel, sitting there on the ratty old couch, hugging himself and giving Ben a mistrustful glare.

Nothing would ever be the same again.

Chapter 7
Winner Takes All

Wrapped in a towel, Kyle was led upstairs to rest and recover from their scene in one of the small, private rooms on the main floor. Kyle lay down on the bed. Ben took a seat beside him, neither of them saying anything. They'd passed Gabriel on the way up, but no words were exchanged and Gabriel, looking angry or hurt or maybe just annoyed, hadn't met Ben's gaze.

"So," Ben began, phrasing his concern with care, "I can't help wondering why that happened. Not that I mind. It just kind of goes against everything I was basing our arrangement around."

He was afraid of scaring Kyle off. There seemed to be no possible way that what happened in the shower hadn't crossed Kyle's sacred boundary lines. The sex had been spectacular, but it hadn't made any sense at all. Sure, there had been the possibility that maybe, after months or years, Kyle might get to a place where sex was not out of the question. But not this early. Not when Ben still felt like they barely knew each other. Not when it felt like Ben's commiseration was actively hurting Kyle.

First, Kyle had changed his mind about his contract. Then on the same *day*, he instigated sex. Did it have anything to do with Dmitri? If it did, the reaction was way out of proportion to the cause.

Did it have anything to do with the way Ben had detected how tenderness and pleasure were scarier than pain for his new submissive? If so, Ben had no clue why, or how, or what to do next.

"You need to talk to me, slave," Ben said more severely, when Kyle didn't even turn to look in Ben's direction, but stayed reclined on his stomach, his face turned to the wall. "These are some big goddamn decisions you're making without explanation, and—"

Kyle finally moved. He pushed up onto his knees, then climbed off the bed, his gaze trained on a cabinet on the far wall rather than Ben. Crossing to it, Kyle retrieved a bottle of lube and tossed it underhand to Ben before returning to the bed, naked. Climbing onto the bed on his knees, Kyle kept his ass tipped up invitingly and lowered his shoulders to the bed, drawing the pillow close to wrap his arms around it while he waited for Ben to act.

"God *dammit*," Ben cursed, bursting with frustration.

Kyle's astoundingly hot ass was right there, open, wet and ready to get fucked. Again.

Don't do it. Don't fucking give in to him. Make him talk. Make him explain and pay some fucking respect.

It shouldn't have been as easy to get under his skin as it was for Kyle. Ben had taken what seemed like countless submissives. Before he worked as a Dom, he was a club promoter. His whole life had been about crafting the enjoyment of those around him. He was always in charge. Everyone else got played, but he stayed above it all, beyond their reach.

Not with Kyle.

From the *start*, all it took was one glance. The side of his face was pressed to that damned pillow and the fucking sad-eyed look he gave Ben snapped his will cleanly, before Ben had even realized it happened. One minute, Ben was sitting there, fuming—mostly at himself. The next, he was climbing onto the bed behind Kyle and opening his pants.

Ben could feel that the damned expression on Kyle's face was still there, though he couldn't actually see it anymore.

Annoyed by everything, Ben yanked his shirt over his head and shoved his pants out of the way hard enough to strain the seams. Then his hands were on Kyle, with minds of their own, and intentions wholly separate from those pinging around inside Ben's head. Rubbing the slight curve of Kyle's hip and squirting some of the lube into his crack, Ben fed Kyle two fingers before he'd had the chance to calm down. As soon as he realized how *good* Kyle felt, in a way it only made Ben angrier.

Typically, he was the one doling out punishments. Not this time.

Kyle was soundly kicking his ass, without much effort at all. It should have been easy to ignore the come-on and act responsibly. Mainly, it was the dichotomy of Ben's expectations that Kyle was straight or a virgin, or simply unwilling to fuck, to the reality of having Kyle effortlessly take from Ben whatever Kyle wanted to claim. The way Kyle had moved in that shower, the subtle gyrations and responses to stimulation indicated that not only was this *not* Kyle's first time with anal sex, he was a fucking *pro*.

And damned if Ben didn't want another piece of that.

"What happened to your damned rules, slave?" Ben complained. It came out sounding more like whining than Ben would have liked. "What happened to the hands-and-dicks-off clause?"

Kyle just tilted his hips a little more, shifted his thighs, drawing Ben's gaze right to Kyle's fucked-loose, rosy knot and Ben's fingers buried in it. Then, Kyle sighed. He fucking *sighed*.

The sound of it sharpened sweetly into an aching moan and that was all Ben's willpower intended to take, it seemed, because he was pressing the head of his cock through that tender opening before he'd realized he pulled his fingers out. Again, there was no condom. Ben only remembered condoms existed after he was halfway inside and moaning with embarrassing candor.

"God, I love your fucking *ass*," Ben groaned unhappily, kneading the muscle of Kyle's behind and rocking into the thrust. "What the fuck is even happening?"

There was a glimmer of a smile. It snagged Ben's wavering attention. So, in response, he guided Kyle upright. Ben sat back on his heels and sat Kyle right down on the rest of Ben's dick. It produced another one of those brain-melting little mewling cries. That, coupled with the frown on Kyle's face, like it hurt in the best kind of way, and the quivering of his thighs, dusted with blond hair, made Ben growl and push to claim and possess.

Fully joined, buried in something forbidden, Ben tried to breathe and calm down. He took hold of Kyle's chin and turned his face to the side to better study it.

"Why are you doing this to me?" Ben demanded. With his left hand, he took firm hold of Kyle's sizable erection and began stroking it. It made him squirm in a fantastic kind of way, practically forcing

Ben to bite Kyle's earlobe just so he didn't spontaneously combust from how hot it was.

"I like you," Kyle said on his next exhale, which twisted around an aching moan. A smile rippled, becoming anguished.

"Well, I don't like *you* very much right now."

Kyle snorted with surprised laughter, his smile coming back. Circling his hips, Kyle alternately rode Ben's fist and his cock. Ben could have watched that all day, but the effect Kyle's motion was having on Ben's body made that impossible. He was so close already, so he folded Kyle forward again, keeping his own body flush to Kyle's back. Kissing him over his shoulder, moaning anew when Kyle's tongue teased at Ben's, Ben pushed and pushed and came with a hard shudder, emptying his load deeply into Kyle's body.

As Ben pumped Kyle faster, sending him racing toward climax, Kyle broke their kiss and seemed to fight the pleasure Ben was giving him. A hint of the sadness came back right before his entire body clenched with orgasm. Panting, shivering, held tightly in Ben's embrace, Kyle was slow to come down, and reluctant to open his eyes.

"Bad kitty," Ben sighed, purged of his fight, riding the wave of bliss that still had his nerve endings firing everywhere. He caressed Kyle's stomach, down his thighs, and rocked lazily against the tight curve of his ass. The more he touched Kyle, the farther his hands roamed and the less he wanted to stop touching him.

They kissed again, for quite a while. Footsteps could be heard beyond the room, pacing up and down the hall.

It would have been easy enough to stay there, and do it all again, but Kyle was exhausted. And Ben had new, additional responsibilities to him now.

"You're not changing the contract again, are you?" Ben said, already knowing it was true.

Kyle shook his head slightly.

"No sex during submission?"

There was hesitation, then a nod.

"But when we're not in a scene..."

Kyle opened his eyes, and they were so blue, they seemed the most vibrant thing in the room, like a vital piece of the world was there, a secret ocean filled with dangerous things.

"Just you," Kyle whispered, quietly and awful enough in its sincerity of trust to drive Ben mad.

"Then these are my rules, slave," Ben warned. "Whether we're in a scene or not. No one touches you without my prior approval and no one else... on this entire fucking *planet*... has you like *this*."

"Okay," Kyle replied, like it was no big deal.

"I'm not kidding. I will find them. I will castrate them. I will take them the fuck apart."

"Yeah, I got it. Okay." He searched Ben's face, for god knew what. "Do you have sex with your other slaves?"

Ben was hyper-aware of how close they were, and how tenderly he was holding Kyle, their breathing synchronized, chests rising and falling together.

"Not like this," he admitted with a self-conscious sort of chuckle. "Only during appointments. No side action."

"Good."

"I'm driving you home," Ben said sternly. "I will help you clean up. I will put you to bed and provide you with something to eat and drink. You will stay in bed and rest until the morning, which is when I will come to get you. Then, we're both going to the clinic to get tested. *Then* we get your car."

"Yes, Sir," Kyle answered with a hint of a happy smile.

It made Ben angry, how happy it made *him* to see it there, in place of that sad-fucking-eyed look.

"Fucking hell," Ben groaned.

If you enjoyed this story, you can sign up for a free membership at ForbiddenFiction and discuss it with other readers and the author at the *Divine Surrender* story page.

Never Happened

For Gabriel Hunter, a professional Dominant, avoiding real intimacy is paramount. Even the cautious love he has for his closest friend — fellow Dominant Ben Knox — is a potential source of further pain. Ben knows all about the shadows in Gabriel's past. Every once in a while, when the opportunity presents itself, Ben can't resist giving Gabriel a sample of what he's been missing. (M/M)

Never Happened

It's late — almost midnight. Since Diadem, a BDSM club, is out in the middle of nowhere, an oasis of debauchery adrift in miles upon miles of farmland, the dark presses in more than it might have otherwise. There's no one around but them and no doubt some wild animals prowling the grounds, searching for sustenance or shelter. They had been understaffed to begin with that day, but now the place is deserted. Mostly.

Running his hands through his dark brown, hair, tousled like he just rolled out of bed, his grey-blue eyes peering out into the gloom, Gabriel Hunter leans over the counter in the kitchenette at the rear of Diadem's main building. His shoulders hunch as the weight of his day and his loneliness bears down on him. He has worked at Diadem in many capacities for years, first as a janitor when he was still under-age and it wasn't entirely legal for him to be there at all, then later as a professional Dominant for hire to Diadem's clientele. Though his slender build and unlikely good looks have always worked against him in trying to gain respect, his attitude and reputation have more than made up the difference.

He can hear movement behind him. That would be Ben Knox and Kyle Ross finishing up.

That evening, Gabriel had assisted Ben — Gabriel's best friend, mentor and, arguably, savior for the past ten years — as he dominated Kyle, a professional submissive, and worked the camera. It wasn't a personal session, just filming for a BDSM video for distribution on their website. Still, watching the other two men interact, the well-earned trust built bit-by-bit between them over time, the closeness they share — Gabriel wants that. More than anything he wants to have that in his life, but it will never happen. His mental walls, which have been protecting him so well, are now more of a hindrance, because how could he ever think of letting anyone get as close to him as Kyle has gotten to Ben? Gabriel can't even imagine trusting someone that much, allowing another man to get that far inside his comfort zone. There'd have to be confessions, truths told. While the walls still stand, barricading Gabriel from the bad things awaiting out there in the world, he remains safer, but painfully on his own. And that sucks.

He takes a swig from his glass, hisses at the burn. There are footsteps behind him.

"Fuck off."

As soon as he grunts the bitter coupling of words, he knows it was the wrong thing to say. Ben, with his naturally curly, trimmed-short hair, his neat, immaculately maintained beard and vibrantly blue, aggravatingly intelligent eyes, comes up behind him, reaching around to grab the tumbler right out of Gabriel's hand. Sniffing its contents, then opening the nearest cabinet to find the bottle, he says pleasantly, "Well, I think we all know what this means. Whip it out."

"Knox," Gabriel complains, trying to shrug Ben off when he wraps his meaty hands around Gabriel's shoulders and starts to rub, kneading the tension away. "Go bang your human fucktoy and leave me alone."

If Ben is in here, Gabriel knows Kyle can't be far away. Gabriel glances around for the little, blond, deceptively-angelic-looking weasel, seeing no signs of him, while Ben sips some of Gabriel's rum and nonchalantly cups Gabriel's crotch through his jeans. By all intents and purposes, it should be weird to be so casually fondled by your best friend, but nothing in their lives is normal anyway, and it hasn't been for as long as they can remember. The rules everyone else likes to play by just don't exist here, between the two professional Dominants.

"Nah," Ben says, eyeing him with a knowing glint in his eye, "You drinking rum, *here*, and bitching like a little cunt, is like finding you naked in my bed with a big, pink bow around your pecker. You've got my attention, sweetheart. Let Benny make it better."

"God, you're not sexy at all when you do that," Gabriel slurs somewhat drunkenly. He takes his booze back from Ben, rocking slightly into Ben's rolling squeezes at the junction of his legs. "And stop that."

"Stop enjoying it," Ben mocks. "Come on, Hunter. This'd be a lot less pathetic if one of us was getting off."

Watching from over Gabriel's right shoulder, Ben studies Gabriel as he recedes farther into his own head, eyes glazing. There's one of two things that come next. If Ben were Trace—Diadem's founder, a Dominant who took Gabriel in when he was a homeless, runaway teen, becoming Gabriel's protector, more family than friend—there would be violence. Trace would basically have to force the orgasm from Gabriel, kicking and yelling. Gabriel likes to let Trace try to test his boundaries, since Trace is trusted so profoundly, but Gabriel doesn't make it easy for him. Even though Ben is definitely *not* Trace, there still might be a fight, but Ben doesn't want to fight Gabriel. Not like that. This has always been their way of coping, sick humor like the rich amber-hued rum in the glass enclosed in Gabriel's fist.

"Drink the rest," Ben coaxes, popping open Gabriel's fly while he's distracted. Kyle is nearby, they both sense it, but can't be bothered with that now. "That's it. Down the hatch."

Gabriel groans a little when it hits his throat, but it rouses him. Some of the scariness leaves his expression, evaporating but leaving a sour note in the air. Ben slips a hand inside Gabriel's boxers and eases him free, bracing for it, waiting for things to turn the corner, like they almost always do. Gabriel knows that the worst thing Ben has ever seen is his best friend reacting to him like he's his rapist. That's why they keep finding themselves here, right here, trying to find a way past it.

Gabriel feels Ben's scrutiny even more keenly than the hand on his cock. Pumping him slowly, perfectly attuned to Gabriel's current, precise level of panic, Ben says softly, "You know Kyle should probably be doing this instead. I could put him in that pink tulle skirt, maybe a wig with pigtails. Think of the video sales, Hunter! You owe it to your customers."

A smile flirts at the edges of Gabriel's lips, "That's horrible. Why do you give me these mental images when—" The rest breaks off on a small cry and Ben shifts closer, tugs harder. Then it's right there, terror like ice water spilling into Gabriel's system. Ben has him between the counter and his body and Gabriel pushes off from the counter with both hands, trying to get more room. Ben is flush to his back, though, his hand locked around Gabriel's dick, manipulating him expertly. Warm breath skates over the side of Gabriel's neck, making him shiver. His best friend's voice in his ear, the most comforting thing in the world, says, "He was pretty sweet down there tonight, wasn't he? You know I fucked him last night? He's so cherry, Gabe. Maybe that's what you need. Slip it to some unassuming twink... one of your subs..."

Gabriel is still fighting. He tries and fails to disguise a scared little sigh that he knows has Ben blistering with rage at the sick fuck that did this to his friend, scarring him so deeply it could never heal. The impulse is there, though, despite how very much Ben knows, to grab Gabriel and restrain him, to take the power away from him and show him how freeing trust can be. It's no mystery why Trace gives in to that, and why Gabriel actively seeks it from him. But if there's anything Gabriel doesn't need, it's someone else looking to take advantage of his vulnerability.

The flesh gripped in Ben's hand is hot and hard. Heat radiates from Gabriel's whole body and the alcohol begins to work on his mind. Tugging Gabriel at a faster pace, simply trying to get him off, Ben is the snake in the garden, hissing words of temptation, winding around and around, then constricting until something breaks.

"How long's it been since you fucked someone that was begging for it?"

"Too damn long," Gabriel grunts.

"What's stopping you?"

Gabriel's head rolls to the side, his face turned away, gasping. He writhes in Ben's grasp, even stiffer now, right on the edge. Shifting his grip, using both hands, arms wound around Gabriel's hips, Ben brings him off in a few more strokes, catching the mess and feeling Gabriel shudder through it.

Without waiting for Gabriel to come down or get freaked out, Ben goes to the sink and rinses his hands. He expects Gabriel to take off

without another word, so Ben is a little startled when, instead, he is shoved back against the wall hard enough to knock the air from his lungs. His head connects with the drywall and, for a second, he sees stars. Once he gets his bearings, the first thing Ben sees is Kyle, all shining blond hair, gorgeous blue eyes and unassuming sweetness on the outside, but dark, dirty and wicked on the inside, standing in the shadows beyond the doorway, watching carefully. The first thing Ben *feels* is Gabriel opening his pants, rolling a rubber onto him.

Cursing, Ben stares up at the ceiling, unwilling or unable to look at Gabriel while he's on his knees, hungrily feeding Ben's dick into his mouth. The whole time, Ben can feel Kyle watching, and not once does Ben move to touch Gabriel in any way. He simply stands there, letting his best friend suck him. He can't really help it when he begins to thrust, because Gabriel has always been good at figuring out what people like, what pushes their buttons. And Ben can't think of anything clever or light-hearted or funny to say. There's not really anything funny about this.

He comes with a hard groan, hips twitching, riding the soft, close heat of Gabriel's mouth. A moment later, Gabriel is on his feet, stalking from the room, right past Kyle. Their shoulders brush. The building's front door slams. Kyle steps into the kitchenette and, from outside, a truck's engine roars to life. Stripping off the soiled condom, Ben tosses it. He takes a few damp paper towels from Kyle to clean up with when Kyle so very helpfully hands some over. Ben murmurs a word of thanks.

"Anything else you need from me tonight, sir?" Kyle asks.

Ben does try to read between the lines of the question, to interpret if Kyle was put off by seeing his Master being intimate with one of the few other men that have also dominated Kyle, but Kyle is the picture of composure and calm. Wondering if Kyle heard everything Ben said to Gabriel, assuming he had, Ben considers his response. He stares back into Kyle's blue eyes, looking for jealousy or feelings of betrayal. Kyle lets him, like he's daring Ben to find some and call him on it.

"No. Go on and take off. I'll see you in a few days."

Kyle nods slowly, looking the faintest bit disappointed. Turning, he heads back into the shadows. Before he gets to the front door, though, Ben calls out, "I don't think I need to tell you that what you saw stays between us. It never happened."

"Yes, sir," is the quiet reply, echoing back through the hall. Then Kyle is gone too, and all Ben is left with is ghosts, and his own restless truths.

If you enjoyed this story, you can sign up for a free membership at ForbiddenFiction and discuss it with other readers and the author at the *Never Happened* story page at http://forbiddenfiction.com/library/story/LK1-1.000015.

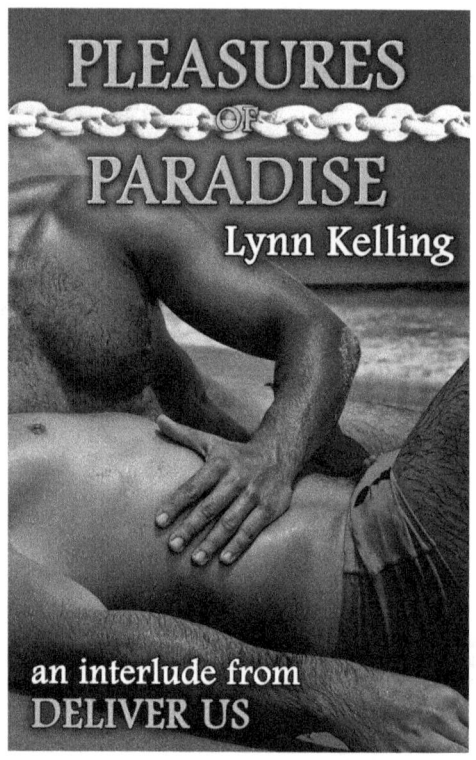

Pleasures of Paradise

To celebrate their two year anniversary, Gabriel Hunter and Darrek Grealey escape to a tropical island in the Florida Keys catering only to Masters and slaves of the BDSM community. The types of gifts Darrek and Gabriel give each other during the trip are vastly different, testing them both even as they fall deeper in love, rediscovering the pleasures of the power dynamic which first caused them to fall in love. As the end of their trip draws near, Gabriel plans a surprise for Darrek unlike anything he's previously faced. Darrek is forced to choose between his instinct to doubt himself and the chance to trust Gabriel in ways he's never dreamed possible. (M/M)

Chapter 1

Sweating It

Covered in a thick layer of sweat from running five miles in the humid heat of the island, over hard dirt paths and shifting sandy expanses, Darrek Grealey savors with a low moan the initial blast of air conditioning coming from the cottage. His long, shoulder-length, sandy brown hair is tied up behind his head, so the cool air feels good on his neck, not to mention every other bit of exposed skin on his body. Wearing only a pair of exercise shorts and sneakers, most of the perspiration covering his body is instantly chilled, cooling him off fast. His skin pebbles with goosebumps and his nipples stiffen tightly as a blissful shiver courses through him.

Opening the door all the way, he steps inside.

Instantly, he's slapped back to reality. His brief moment of respite, brought by the refreshing temperature change, is ended abruptly when he sees his partner, Gabriel Hunter, standing in the hall. Gabriel's chiseled biceps are on display with his arms folded over his lean, toned chest. His stern expression, rigid with displeasure, is both beautiful and terrible to behold as his grey-blue eyes burn brightly with a cold fire. His short, dark brown hair is tousled in a sexy but maddeningly intentional way and, as usual, Darrek gets one glimpse of Gabriel's full lips, pressed together tightly, and just wants to suck on them.

There's only one thing he can do. The rules are clear.

Exhausted enough to be grateful for not being expected to decide on his course of action, Darrek drops to his knees instinctively. Then, he turns his face up. Warm, brown eyes lock on to Gabriel, as Darrek clasps his hands behind his back as best he can; his sweat-drenched shirt is balled up in one fist. After spending a solid hour in the gym doing curls, bench presses, pull-ups, push-ups, sit-ups, squats—the whole nine—he'd hit the trails for his daily run. It's been his routine for weeks now.

Plus there's the new diet, managed entirely by Gabriel. Darrek eats and drinks only what Gabriel tells him to—nothing else. Protein shakes, lots of carbs before each run, and mostly fresh fruit and vegetables later. It has slimmed him down, but Darrek misses things like cheese and dessert, which he hasn't tasted in months, if you don't count the chocolate sauce he'd carefully licked off of Gabriel's cock a few weeks ago. That brief indulgence of sugary sweetness was heaven. The whole vacation has been somewhat heavenly. Darrek knows that missing things like dairy and sweets only makes them that much more of an appreciated reward when he *does* get them.

These memories of food dance in his head as another drip of sweat rolls down the side of his nose to his upper lip, catching there. Worn out, needing a shower like air, feeling gross, slimy, and smelly, Darrek kneels before Gabriel. Slowly, his breathing regulates. His hands slip twice before he gets a better grip on his wrist to stay in the pose. The muscles in his legs burn, stiff as granite from the exertion of running. Gabriel waits patiently as Darrek gets settled and wonders about the reason why he's been stopped mere inches from the bathroom door where his desperately desired shower awaits him. But it's not Darrek's place to ask, so he doesn't even consider it.

Of course, if it was Saturday instead of Thursday, it'd be a whole different story. As soon as he had come through the door, Darrek would have tackled Gabriel to the bed and easily overpowered him. While Darrek rubbed his sweaty self all over him, ignoring every protest and complaint, he would have tickled out the reason why what Gabriel wants to say can't wait ten more minutes until Darrek doesn't stink to high heaven anymore.

But it's not Saturday, so Darrek is nothing but obedient and attentive as he follows the rules submissively.

"Your shirt is off. Why is your shirt off?" Gabriel demands in a clipped, displeased tone of voice.

Saturday's answer: 'Because it was stuck to me like plastic wrap, and not in a fun, kinky sort of way either and I was literally going to die of discomfort if I didn't peel the damn thing off of me, now move your pretty ass so I can take my shower, goddammit.'

Thursday's answer: "I'm sorry, sir. It's especially humid today and I was trying to cool off before I got lightheaded."

Gabriel considers this with one finger tapping the seam of his pursed lips, "And what is the correct behavior in that type of circumstance?"

"To call you and ask for permission to disrobe, sir."

There are free phones located all over the island specifically for the purpose of keeping its visitors in touch with each other. Really, Darrek has no excuse. He hadn't brought his cell but that doesn't matter.

"Damn right. You were out there giving a free show to the whole fucking island, and I don't appreciate you displaying my property without consent."

Slightly aggravated, Darrek clenches his jaw. It's a very subtle, slight reaction, but Gabriel notices it like Darrek shouted at him instead. With a prolonged gaze down at Darrek's loose, grey shorts, which hang from his narrow hips, Gabriel watches as they slowly become tented in the front after the brief reference to Darrek's body being Gabriel's property. The reason for his arousal is more complicated than that, though. Really, Darrek is getting off on Gabriel's anger and the implied threat of retribution. Intentionally playing right into Darrek's unspoken but glaringly obvious fantasy, Gabriel narrows his eyes and steps forward.

"I'm sorry, *slave*, do you have a problem with that?" Gabriel growls, adding, "And I don't believe I gave you permission to get an erection either."

With a frustrated little grunt, Darrek looks pointedly up at the ceiling, trying to will away his interest. It doesn't really work.

It's become commonplace for Darrek to accompany Gabriel to the beach wearing only a collar and leash around his neck, and nothing else, so Darrek finds it hilarious in a dry sort of way for his Master to get so upset over the removal of a shirt on the short, mostly-enclosed walk back to the cottage from the submissives-only exercise room. It means that Gabriel is looking for an excuse to punish his slave, which Darrek doesn't really mind at all. It's more the principle of the thing.

He'd be throwing Gabriel his best bitchface, with a hand braced on his hip, gesturing dramatically with the other if it was Saturday. Since it's not, he's willing to push the issue slightly by hinting at his annoyance, but there's no way he'd do anything more extreme to get himself in hotter water than is necessary.

Counting the hours until he has freedom once more to speak his mind, already planning what he's going to do to Gabriel as payback for this, he tries not to hope too hard for a particularly creative punishment. Darrek puts on what he hopes is an apologetic frown and murmurs, "I'm sorry, Master. You're right. It's just so difficult to contain myself when I'm around you. And no, I don't have a problem, sir. I'll make sure I no longer make the mistake of displaying your property without permission."

Gabriel reaches out and scratches lightly over Darrek's chest, through slick, salty perspiration, leaving pink trails over his sternum, left pectoral muscle and areola before flicking briefly over his pebbled nipple. "Who does this belong to? Say it."

"It belongs to you. I belong to you, Master. Body and soul," Darrek recites automatically, shivering a little at the touch.

"Does it belong to *you*? Can you do whatever the fuck you want with this, such as whore yourself out to anyone who wants to take a look?"

"No, of course not, sir. Would you like to punish me for my brashness?"

"Would you like that, slave?"

"Yes, sir. Please."

"Very well. Take your shower. You smell like a wet dog. Then meet me in the living quarters for your punishment."

"Thank you, sir. Is there any special preparation you would like me to make?"

"Not this time, but thank you for asking. Oh, but don't touch your cock except to clean it, understand?"

"Yes, sir."

"Would you like some water to drink?"

"Fuck yes," Darrek moans, adding as an afterthought, "Thank you, Master."

"You're welcome, baby," Gabriel smiles, handing over an ice cold liter of spring water.

Darrek moans again, even louder, and takes a drink before he even stands. He struggles to his feet with Gabriel's help as his muscles threaten to knot up. Taking Darrek's elbow, Gabriel hoists him up. There are red marks on Darrek's knees and shins from the tile floor. When Darrek sways and grabs the doorway for support, Gabriel frowns and says, "I'll get you something to eat. Call for me if you feel lightheaded. You need me to come in there with you?"

"Nah. M'okay," Darrek smiles tiredly.

Chapter 2
Crossing the Line

The luxury and quiet splendor of the bathroom draws him in. Darrek tries to really enjoy it while he still can, since this is their last week of vacation. In a few days, they'll be back at home, back to work. Gabriel will be fully engulfed in the demanding task of jump-starting his photography business after their three-month-long holiday. For his part, Darrek will be back to filling his back-logged carpentry orders and working with his construction crew again.

As he stares at himself reflected in the massive, wall-sized mirror above the marble counter of the vanity, Darrek reminds himself to enjoy each moment while he can. There's no telling what waits for them back home. Concern swells and then dissolves away with effort. There's no point in worrying yet, he tells himself. It would only spoil what little alone-time he has left with Gabriel.

Soft light filters in through the high, stained glass windows, coupled with the recessed lighting and small twin sconces by the vanity, reflecting off of porcelain, glass, and marble. The slick sweat dripping down Darrek's newly chiseled body glistens. He knows he looks good, better than he ever has, in fact. It makes the hard work of maintaining his physique worth it. All he wants is to be everything Gabriel could want him to be. It's all for Gabriel—Darrek's anniversary gift to him; a gift of himself—healthy, immaculate, and eager to submit in every way imaginable. Gabriel's gift had been the vacation itself. Three months in paradise; a private island in the Florida Keys devoted to providing services and facilities for those living a twenty-four/seven Dominant/submissive lifestyle.

The picture-perfect, white, expansive beaches, the gourmet restaurants, the decked-out training facilities, the sprawling, decadent pools, the playrooms and supplies available—every facility is tailored specifically for their unique needs. If they want privacy, they can have it, but if Gabriel wants to show off his slave, that can happen, too. If Gabriel wants Darrek to be bound and blindfolded during dinner service in the formal dining room, shackled on his knees beside Gabriel's chair or tied securely to his own while they're surrounded by a roomful of other diners, then that can happen, no questions asked.

Two years. They've been committed to each other for two years. A smile lights Darrek's face. He turns the water on in the two-person shower and waits for it to get warm. The Jacuzzi looks tempting but that'll have to wait. It would help to soothe his overtaxed muscles, but he wants to get food in his now-empty stomach and not take too long getting ready.

Steam begins to rise in the glass-enclosed shower stall. He steps under the spray and moans, pushing his hands back through his long, thick, sun-lightened brown hair, combing it back from his face, getting it wet. His fingers slide easily through the strands, combing over his scalp. The jets of hot water blast his skin clean, beating against it, the heat of it bringing blood to the surface, the force of it massaging away some of his aches.

One of the reasons they decided to take this trip and agree to such a long stretch of time as purely Master and slave is that their relationship more and more has veered away from the lifestyle. It was the way they met—as Master and slave. But, the more time has passed, the more full-bodied their relationship has become. BDSM sometimes seems like a luxury they don't have the time or energy to indulge in. The demands of work and home take over.

So, they both agreed it was worth the cost to take time away, only for themselves and each other, to reconnect as they first did. Every day but Saturday, Darrek's day off, they are, above all else, Master and slave. Every day but Saturday, Gabriel makes the rules and Darrek has the glorious freedom from any responsibility other than following Gabriel's rules. On Saturday, however, all bets are off. Darrek can do whatever he wants, within reason. Strangely enough, he usually plays by the rules on Saturdays, too. It's just part of his nature to derive pleasure and comfort from being Gabriel's submissive. He owns the role with pride, always.

Soap suds slip down Darrek's body, over each and every muscle, down his bulging chest and arms, his rock-hard abs, his tight glutes and his burning thighs. The bubbles feel lighter than silk, the most insubstantial little tickle, even as the humidity and force of the water against the back of his neck relaxes him. It's perfect.

He cleans everywhere, scrubbing, using his loofah to exfoliate, his douching bulb, his razor to touch up any rough spots, though he's been waxed regularly by Gabriel — his arms, chest, back, and genitals. There's a microdermabrasion cream he applies to his face, to buff away dirt and dead skin cells. Once he's rinsed clean, he shuts off the water and grabs one of the big, fluffy, white towels, patting his face dry then wrapping it around his waist. At the sink, he moisturizes his skin and blows out his hair. Every detail is important when trying to impress a Dominant with discriminating tastes.

It's been quite a head-trip to be surrounded by other Dominants, Dominatrixes, and submissives, having to be 'on' all the time, and be ready for whatever Gabriel wants to dish out. It's made Darrek feel part of a community much larger than the small circle of friends awaiting them back home, and the world of Diadem, where Gabriel learned the arts of power, pleasure, trust, and control. To be able to own his particular desires publicly, without fear of harsh judgment or misunderstanding, has been profoundly liberating. This summer has been the best, most exciting time of Darrek's life. He feels loved exqui-sitely, completely. He's done things and had things done to him that he's never dreamed of indulging in before. Every day is something new — an adventure or surprisingly unique fantasy brought to life.

Once in a while, though, amidst paradise and its splendor, the rules need to bend. Gabriel doesn't like to ask for things on Darrek's free day, but sometimes he has to. Similarly, if Darrek needs to say something to Gabriel, outside the context of their rules or protocol, they wanted to devise a comfortable way for him to do so.

The way they have come to handle those instances is to pass notes. They write what they need to say, fold it up, and slip it into the other's hand. Darrek has only used this communication technique once, after a few days on the beach and witnessing the way everyone was staring at him. Gabriel had warned him in advance that the following day he would be bringing Darrek to the beach nude, his thick brown leather collar his only attire. The night before, Darrek had scrawled a note and given it to Gabriel, asking for a blindfold, too. He didn't want to see everyone's eyes on him; he only wanted to feel them looking. It had been too much, seeing who was ogling his body—older men and women, beautiful young female submissives, and gorgeous, hulking men groping him with only their eyes, being afforded the privilege only because Gabriel permitted it, knowing that they could look at whatever they wanted to, imagining the dirty, kinky things he and Gabriel do together behind closed doors, but knowing all the while that Gabriel is the only one permitted to touch.

He didn't even explain why he needed the blindfold. He didn't have to. Gabriel understood. Of course he did. So, Darrek got his wish. It made him infinitely more comfortable, having his sense of sight taken from him. It got him hotter, too. Imagining something can be so much sexier than the reality. Something that could easily have turned creepy and unsettling stayed controlled, and manageable.

Eventually, after many weeks, Darrek was able to go to the beach without the blindfold, but it was a gradual process he chose to endure, inching his personal boundary lines a little farther each time he went out.

Darrek pulls off the towel, overhands it into the hamper, and smiles as he's drawn from the sanctuary of the bathroom by the heavenly scent of eggs, ham, and coffee.

"Mmm...oh *wow*," he groans, stalking over to the counter where the hot, freshly prepared food has been set out for him already by Gabriel, who is washing his hands and grinning by the sink. "Thank you."

"You're welcome. Sit. Eat."

Darrek points at the stool, his eyebrows raised in question.

"Yes, sit on the stool. I'm not going to make you sit on the floor after all of that. I'm ordering you to ease up a little on the workouts if they're taking that much out of you. I want you with some energy leftover after them."

"Yes, sir. Okay," Darrek mumbles around a mouthful of food before moaning loudly at the taste. "Oh my god, this is so good. This is amazing. I love you."

"I love you, too." Gabriel leans against the opposite side of the counter, watching Darrek's pleasure as he eats. "Your body is fucking sick. You're so beautiful, Dare, it almost hurts to look at you. Well, no, it does literally hurt, because I'm walking around with blue balls all day, especially when I get to take you out and show you off."

Darrek stops in mid-chew, his expression growing warier by the second. He glances down at the omelet and coffee prepared so carefully for him, Gabriel's buttery praise ringing in his ears. One thing is certain. Gabriel is up to something. He's softening Darrek up before the blow.

Never having been very good at masking his thoughts, Darrek tenses. His apprehension only grows when Gabriel seems to zero in on it, his plump, suckable lips curling into a wicked grin as he chuckles. Darrek continues eating, but begins to feel more like a squirrel fearfully guarding its nut. As soon as the plate is clean and the last drop of delicious coffee is sliding down Darrek's throat, Gabriel moves around the counter, walking from the kitchen into their living space.

The bedroom adjoins the sitting area, and Darrek dutifully follows Gabriel when he walks over to the bed. There seems to be something laying on the duvet, but covered by a black scarf. With his heart pounding, Darrek's eyes grow wider when Gabriel pulls the scarf away and says, "I want you to wear something special for me today. I ordered this weeks ago. It just came in this morning when you were on your run."

On the bed, laid out so nicely, is a shimmery, sleek, baby-pink-hued, little bathing bikini with an equally small, shear ruffled mini-skirt attached. Darrek is not even sure he can fit his junk into it, let alone his ass. Maybe that's the point. But even worse is the body glitter, pink lipstick and purple eyeliner sitting there beside the suit. And worst of all....

Gabriel picks up two hair elastics the same color as the suit, twirling them on a finger. "I'm going to put these in your hair. Pigtails," Gabriel beams.

"Tundra," Darrek blurts.

The safeword hangs for a moment in the air between them. For Darrek, it came out instinctively. Still, he's a little surprised to hear himself use it.

Slowly, Gabriel nods. He sets down the elastics and loses the smile, growing serious instead as he considers Darrek's body language and facial expression. "Okay," Gabriel says, "Can you talk to me about what you're feeling? This is too much?"

"Yes," Darrek says quickly, without really thinking about that answer either.

"Why? Help me understand where you're coming from. You know my job is to challenge you in ways that I think you'll enjoy and will be rewarding in the end, so can you tell me what it is about this that's over the line? Just because... I didn't think this would be a trigger for you."

After thinking about it for a second, Darrek replies, "I'm not sure why."

"Is it just the pigtails or the whole outfit?" Gabriel asks, frowning and planting his hands on his hips. He looks over the things he'd set out like he's trying to find the one thing that's triggering Darrek, but Darrek's not sure it's that simple. Even just thinking about the reasons why he might be uncomfortable makes him uncomfortable.

He decides that maybe Gabriel is right, and talking through it might help him understand where the reflexive reaction to say no is coming from.

"It makes me uncomfortable," Darrek starts to say, feeling like he's tripping over the words.

"What does?" Gabriel asks leadingly. "Uncomfortable in what way?"

"Um, I guess because it would be really embarrassing to be seen like that."

"Why would it be really embarrassing?"

Darrek can feel it, like every time he takes another step closer to the reason why he feels the way he feels, Gabriel finds the exact, right spot to push to get Darrek to go a little farther forward. It's strange, because he's fairly sure it's a path he'd never be able to walk on his own, without his Master's guidance. He'd have just avoided it entirely. But now that he's on the path, he's not sure how to get off of it, or if he even wants to anymore. More than being afraid, he kind of wants to know where his instinctive feelings are coming from, too. Deep down, beneath it all, he's always wanted to know why he has such conflicting feelings about so many things of a sexual or intimate nature. Since he's been young, he's always reacted without questioning his actions. Maybe that hasn't been the right approach at all.

"Don't over-think it," Gabriel suggests. "Just say the first thing that comes into your head."

"My dad wouldn't like it," Darrek says. Then, right away, he feels strongly taken aback. Somewhat introspectively, he murmurs, "Whoa, that's weird. I don't know why... I mean, it's not like he's here, or he'd know what I was doing. Why the hell do I care what my dad thinks?"

Frantically, Darrek searches through his mental inventory of recent, past decisions he's made concerning his sexual behavior, to try to see if his dad has played a part in those as well. It's a disturbing thing to think about.

Gabriel looks up at Darrek beseechingly with his strikingly pale eyes ringed with naturally thick, dark eyelashes.

"Keep going, Dare," Gabriel encourages. "You're doing great."

"He'd want me to feel like it'd be sinful and disgusting to dress like that. Men don't dress that way. Not in private. Not in public."

"But how do *you* feel about it? Your dad doesn't get a say in how you feel."

"I guess I'd be afraid people would laugh at me."

"Who cares what people do? Think about where we are, Dare. If there's anywhere in the world free of judgment, it's here. No one hurts you. No one gets close to you or even sees you without my say so. And you trust me to take care of you, right? I'm *always* going to be taking care of you, no matter the circumstances."

Darrek runs the side of his index finger over his lip, looking at the outfit. He tries to push away all of the thoughts about his father, and the fears about being judged, just in order to see what's hidden underneath. It's a place he's never investigated before.

He thinks about all of the positions, techniques, and toys Gabriel has used with him, helping him find his boundary lines and limits. What's so scary about a weird bathing suit anyway? It's not going to cause physical pain. It's just an outfit.

He looks up at Gabriel, then, trying to understand him, too. It was Gabriel's idea to suggest this. He'd planned it in detail, ahead of time.

This wasn't a whim by any stretch of the imagination. Gabriel had reasons why he wanted this.

He wanders a few steps away from the bed, in their temporary home which they've made use of in countless ways, trying things Darrek never thought he'd be brave enough to try. He takes a deep breath and comes back to the bed. Gabriel is still beside it, watching Darrek with concern, love, and endless patience. Then, Darrek asks him, "Why are you asking me to do this? What's your motivation if it's not to make me feel stupid?"

"I would *never* try to make you feel stupid, Dare," Gabriel says tenderly. He walks up to Darrek and lays a hand on Darrek's chest, caressing him, then presses a kiss to Darrek's shoulder and folds him into a hug. Darrek is only too happy to return it, circling his arms around Gabriel's smaller form. "You want the truth?"

"Yeah. Please. All of it."

"Well, the truth is I thought you'd look really fucking hot with your huge, ripped, perfect body and only that suit to cover it up. And I can't explain how you look so sexy with your hair tied up, but you do. So part of my motivation was selfish, clearly. But I also thought trusting me like this, and doing something like this, which we haven't tried before, ever, might open up new possibilities to you. You respond really well to submitting and being made vulnerable, but you're getting used to a lot of the techniques we've been using these past two years. They don't challenge you like they used to. I figured it was time for something new. That's the truth. But I'll think of something else, okay?"

Gabriel glances around the room, as if searching for ideas. Darrek can't stop looking at the suit, though. It's too garish, too ridiculous.

The more Gabriel scans the small space, trying to brainstorm under pressure in order to ease Darrek's fret, the more Darrek realizes Gabriel isn't making eye contact with him anymore.

"Gabe?"

"Hmm?" Gabriel hums, not looking up into Darrek's eyes.

"Look at me."

With a heavy sigh, Gabriel raises his gaze, and promptly runs a hand over his mouth. He begins to blush a fierce red.

"What?" Darrek laughs a little, amazed by what he's seeing. Gabriel never gets embarrassed. Not like this, not without a really good reason. "Why the heck are you blushing? What aren't you telling me? That wasn't the truth?"

"No, it was the truth," Gabriel murmurs, trying to dodge eye contact again. "Don't mind me. It doesn't matter, okay? Just give me a minute to think. Is there anything you're in the mood for?"

"Gabe," Darrek repeats. "You have to talk to me, too. I'm not a mind reader either."

"It doesn't matter," Gabriel echoes, blushing even pinker. It's astonishingly cute, Darrek decides, especially when Gabriel tries to compensate for his embarrassment by standing in a more manly way, clearing his throat and furrowing his brow.

"Tell me!" Darrek laughs. "It matters to me. *You* matter to me."

"It's stupid."

"Let me be the judge of that. This is us being honest, right? That's what we're doing here? So, be honest. I was really honest with *you*."

Gabriel groans and runs his hand over his face again. "I didn't just buy *one*."

"One what?"

"Pink, frilly, sparkly bikini," Gabriel confesses on a defeated sigh.

"You got me *two of them*? Why would you…. Oh. Oh my god. Oh my *god*!"

Gabriel shoots Darrek a stern look of warning, and chews on his lip as he fidgets uncomfortably.

"Say it. You have to say it," Darrek tells him.

"Oh really, slave? I *have to*?"

"Can I see it? Oh my god, I want to see it."

"What? Why? It's the same. It's just… smaller."

"Oh my god!"

There's something about seeing Gabriel in that flustered state, overwhelmingly embarrassed and self-conscious, just at the idea of talking about buying himself one of the silly bikinis. It does strange things to affect Darrek's previously resolved decision. Gabriel looks even more disturbed by the idea of wearing his own frilly bikini, yet he bought it anyway.

Because he thought Darrek might enjoy it.

"Oh my god," Darrek says more softly, becoming, quickly, unspeakably turned on.

"Stop saying that, please," Gabriel beseeches.

"You would really wear that for me?" Darrek asks quietly.

Gabriel sighs. He raises his eyes to look right at Darrek, and it feels suddenly like the floor has dropped out from under them.

"Fuck," Darrek breathes. "You would."

He tries not to be as excited about the prospect of that as he feels, but it's almost as if he's been zapped with electricity. Darrek's whole body starts to light up. He starts to pace, just to blow off steam, to shake off the energizing sensation, but now he *really* can't stop looking at the bikini.

"Okay," Darrek says after a moment.

"Okay," Gabriel agrees, exhaling heavily and seeming relieved. "So what are you in the mood to do, then?"

"No, um," Darrek says softly, fumbling, feeling awkward. "I mean *okay.*"

"Yeah, I heard you," Gabriel starts, then starts to understand why Darrek has such a funny look on his face. "Wait, you mean *okay?*"

"Yeah, okay. I trust you. Let's do it."

"Do this?" Gabriel asks to clarify, pointing at the suit.

"Yeah. If I agree to this today, and, like, balls to the wall commit to it and let you call the shots, then I want you to wear yours on Saturday."

"Okay," Gabriel nods. "You're sure?"

"Oh, I'm sure," Darrek assures him while doing an astonishingly poor job of containing his raging libido. "I love you, by the way. A *lot.*"

"I love you, too," Gabriel smiles.

Chapter 3
Dolled Up

"Christ, you're such a control freak," Darrek complains from his seat at the vanity in the cottage's bathroom. Gabriel stands behind him, a horsehair brush in one hand, pink hair elastics stretched around the fingers of the other as he gathers half of Darrek's hair and twists it tightly. One of the elastics snaps into place, wound around three times. Since Darrek's hair isn't long enough to braid, the ponytails on either side of his head will have to do.

Brushing the small puff of hair, teasing Darrek's pigtail to fullness, Gabriel squints. "What was that, slave?"

Darrek lifts both hands, palm up, raising his eyebrows and gesturing wildly.

"I'm waiting, smartass."

"You won't even let me do my own hair! Do you know how that makes me feel?"

"Like a pretty princess, I bet. And a spoiled one, too. Now how about we lose the attitude before I decide you need a lesson in manners?"

Darrek claps his mouth shut, his reflection looking absolutely mortified as Gabriel twists the other half of Darrek's long, shining hair into the other ponytail. Darrek hasn't once raised his eyes to look at himself in the mirror, his posture slouched as his body language conveys his intense discomfort. Gabriel decides they need to work on that a little. When they'd first come into the bathroom to begin the scene, at first Darrek couldn't keep his eyes off of Gabriel, and Gabriel is pretty sure he could figure out what his slave was fantasizing about. But, the farther along they get into Darrek's transformation, the more Darrek seems to focus on himself rather than what Saturday will bring.

That's fine, but Gabriel needs Darrek to understand who's in control. Gabriel also needs Darrek in the moment, experiencing sensations instead of getting lost in his head where there are things which could hurt him.

"Sit up straight. Chin up. Now."

Darrek obeys, his spine going as straight as a metal rod, clasping the sides of the chair and tilting his jaw. Eyes stubbornly downcast, he exhales softly when Gabriel leans in and places a single, delicate kiss to the side of his face, watching avidly in the mirror all the while.

It's better than Gabriel hoped it would be. Darrek's chest and arms are covered in millions of shimmering metallic flecks that catch the light. His lips are bubblegum pink and wet with the gloss. But most of all it's Darrek's attitude under the snarky defiance that stiffens Gabriel's dick. He really is relinquishing all power to his Master, Gabriel observes. Even though the makeup and hairdo are fucking with his head, being dressed up like a girl for Gabriel's amusement, none of Darrek's usual fight is there. Instead, he's surrendering to what's happening. Vulnerability, even timidity can be found in the curl of Darrek's lips, the color high in his cheeks, and the energy he puts out. For Gabriel, it's incredibly, intoxicatingly sexy.

There's not much that can make Darrek bashful, not anymore, so Gabriel intends to play it for all it's worth. He realizes he's asking a lot of his lover. The fact that Darrek used his safeword right away has alerted Gabriel that he needs to walk a fine line, not to mention the feelings stirred up about Darrek's abusive asshole of a father. It's not Gabriel's intent to hurt Darrek's feelings, or ask him to do something he'll later regret. He simply wants to test Darrek's ability to trust, and to savor his dutiful slave's fleeting, utterly irresistible vulnerability.

Beside Darrek's ear, Gabriel asks in his gravelly voice while trailing the back of a finger down Darrek's spine, "Do you know what I want?"

"No, sir," Darrek murmurs through gritted teeth.

"Guess."

"For me to get dressed in my suit?"

Gabriel scans the countertop, laden with creams, powders, lotions, lubricants, soaps and anything else they could need. His gaze fixes on one thing in particular, and an idea springs to mind. He grins.

"No. Not yet. I intend to use you before we leave. When we go out there, and everyone looks at you, I want you to be my girl in every sense. I want you dripping wet; your tight, hot little hole stretched out and loose, rubbed a rosy pink from my cock riding you hard. You're gonna feel me where I fucked you open. You're gonna feel it with every fucking step, every movement. After I shoot my come in your ass, I'm going to stick a nice, thick plug in you to keep it there, so that whenever I feel like fucking my girl again, you'll be juicy and begging me to give you more."

Gabriel's lips drag lightly over Darrek's jaw in an open-mouth kiss, and Darrek whispers shakily, *begging*, "Please."

Chuckling, Gabriel drops a hand to Darrek's lap, wrapping his slowly swelling hard-on in a palm. "Oh, you like that, do ya, sweetheart? All that dirty talk is making your pussy wet?"

Setting his jaw, Darrek swallows a grunt when Gabriel strokes him lightly. In seconds he's fully erect. The please was a necessary request for permission, knowing he'd be scolded for not voicing it, especially after the reprimand earlier than morning. He has to answer, but he almost can't. Hesitating longer than is wise, Darrek eventually confesses, "Yes, I like it."

"Say it."

Gabriel can practically see the battle raging inside Darrek over his pride, and he marvels at it.

"*Say it.*"

Darrek does say it, but it's spoken very quietly.

"What was that? I couldn't hear you."

"I said, it makes me wet."

Gabriel directs a sharp, open-handed slap to the underside of Darrek's cock. Gasping, Darrek masters his reaction and bows his head.

"No. Chin *up*. Let's try this again, shall we, princess?"

Darrek forces his chin up, his eyes still downcast, and growls back in his throat. Then he manages, "It makes my pussy wet."

"Much better," Gabriel breathes, squeezing once up Darrek, root to crown, milking a few drops from his slit. Darrek tilts his hips slightly, wriggling on the seat. "You know, all of this defiance is just turning me on even more. You're giving me lots of reasons to make you behave. Is that your plan? To put up a fight so I have to find ways to take all that fight out of you?"

Before Darrek can respond, Gabriel lets him go and turns his back to Darrek, grabbing what he needs from the counter and saying, "Go lie on the bed. You have exactly one minute and one minute only to stretch yourself open for me, so be efficient. Go."

Gabriel fills his mouth with the spearmint mouthwash as soon as Darrek is gone, rinsing with it for as long as he can stand before spitting it out, only to do it again.

When he emerges from the bathroom, crossing quickly to the bed where Darrek lies on his back with his right arm stretched down between his legs and two hurriedly lubed fingers stuffed up his hole, Gabriel doesn't speak. He just comes right at Darrek, leans down over him between his fallen-open legs, takes him in hand, and touches Darrek's cock to his tongue. Closing his lips around the tip, Gabriel hollows his cheeks, sucking him tightly as he feeds Darrek slowly back.

"*Ahhh*! Fuck!" Darrek yelps and then hisses through gritted teeth at the tingling burn from the mouthwash, making one last effort to coax his inner muscles loose as Gabriel curls his tongue around his shaft, easing back now to roll his tongue over the head. Pulling off with a slurp, Gabriel shifts lower, taking hold around the base of Darrek's sac and guiding his balls to his mouth. Licking over them, spreading minty alcohol-tinged saliva over the sensitive skin, Gabriel covers it evenly before going back to blowing him. "You fucker. Goddamn you. Fucking mouthwash."

Humming in agreement, Gabriel's head bobs as he sucks. Darrek's balls, his whole dick—Gabriel knows they must be covered in icy fire.

"*Shit*. Stop. I'm gonna come. Please! Master, please!"

"Already?" Gabriel asks, pulling off with a pop, his lips wet. "Jesus. That's pathetic."

"It's fucking tingling everywhere! It's not stopping. *Fuck*, it's not stopping!" Darrek brings the inside of his forearm to his mouth and bites down on it to distract himself as his orgasm threatens to explode through the tip of his cock. Gabriel watches Darrek's dick twitch, his balls drawn up tightly to his body.

With an iron grip, Gabriel squeezes around the base of Darrek's genitals. Staring coolly down at his slave, Gabriel watches avidly as Darrek whimpers and bites down on his arm again, growling into the now-bruised flesh and bucking wildly into Gabriel's grip.

"Stop damaging my property, slave," Gabriel scolds. "Hands at your sides."

Reluctantly, eyes rolling back, teeth gritted, Darrek shudders. He forces his arms down parallel to his body. His hands clench and unclench repeatedly, quickly, as Darrek fights against both his body's need to come and Gabriel's hand preventing it. Writhing but unable to escape Gabriel's fist locked around his sensitive organs, delightfully stimulated by the mouthwash, Darrek tries to take a breath even as Gabriel squeezes tighter.

"Stay still. Stop moving and take it."

Darrek minimizes his movements, regaining control of himself. Slowly, he masters the panic. The breath tears from his nostrils. They flare as he sucks in oxygen. He's watching Gabriel through his lowered eyelashes as Gabriel bends down and extends his tongue, licking the head of Darrek's dick in a long stripe, rolling the wet, flattened muscle over it. Then, Gabriel does it again before suckling, watching Darrek all the while. Darrek's swollen cock jumps, straining. He growls back in his throat and vibrates, doing everything he can to be still and not fight it.

"It's creeping down your slit, isn't it? Sizzling the inside of your cock, too."

Darrek only growls and blows out a breath.

"Legs up and back," Gabriel instructs. Darrek opens his eyes and gazes down the length of his body, half-swallowing startled little husky cries. He obeys instinctively, Gabriel is pleased to see, drawing his legs back as Gabriel frees his own cock and touches the head to his slave's hole. Putting steady pressure there, he enters Darrek gradually. Darrek's body is clamped up tightly as he continues to struggle with the denial of his orgasm and the overwhelming cold and hot sensation from the mouthwash acting on the delicate tissues of his penis and testicles. "Good... very good," Gabriel rasps, groaning thickly as Darrek's ass swallows him up. "Fuck you're tight."

Darrek blows out a thick breath through his mouth, inhales more air, then holds it while Gabriel gives him a moment to adjust to the burn of the stretch. Even though Darrek's tensed and clenched, Gabriel proceeds to violate his slave anyway, stuffing him full as his grip shifts on Darrek's genitals, squeezing more of him, then letting go in little pulses only to lock up again. Gabriel starts to move inside of him, riding him with shallow but sharp thrusts. Darrek's hands grab fistfuls of the bedding. He's probably wishing for restraints but Gabriel is enjoying Darrek's battle for control too much to make it easier on him like that.

"Relax your hands," Gabriel growls.

Darrek roars his complaint but complies. The tension moves to his feet as they flex and arch. Gabriel pumps his hips, taking Darrek more deeply, while squeezing Darrek's dick with a hand.

Gabriel's breathing roughens, sweat breaks out on his brow. Bracing one hand on Darrek's right foot, Gabriel presses the leg to open up his position as he pounds Darrek's ass raw, not holding anything back. He lets Darrek's dick go and quickly folds his balls up in his palm instead, pulling on them and squeezing around them hard enough to hurt.

Darrek's hands chase over the bed for a moment, seeking for purchase, but finds nothing more substantial to hold on to and ground himself with than a handful of soft bedding. He breathes out all of the air in his lungs and hesitates to draw another breath. The delayed orgasm chases up on him again, underneath the pain, overtaking it quickly. Gabriel sees it happen in the quiver of his slave's muscles.

"Don't come. I mean it. Don't," Gabriel warns.

A low, extended, keening whimper slips from Darrek. His mouth works against the breath that won't come. Gabriel pulls harder on Darrek's sac and Darrek's hips follow up in that direction to relieve the pressure.

"Breathe," Gabriel tells him angrily. His hand twists around without letting go of Darrek's balls, eliciting a sharp little cry. Lower, thickly, Gabriel moans, "Oh my god..."

With a few tight slaps of his hips against Darrek's ass, Gabriel unloads as Darrek roughly gulps down air once and then again.

"Good, baby. Just breathe. I've gotcha," Gabriel promises.

Groaning, eyelashes fluttering, sweating and glittering, Darrek is strung tight as a bow but begins to breathe more evenly. When the last drop of come has been wrung from Gabriel, he slowly withdraws, leaving Darrek gaping and rubbed-pink.

"Good, keep those feet up," Gabriel tells him, only connected to him now by the hand like a vise on Darrek's balls. "Can I let go of you?"

For a long moment, Darrek doesn't answer, so Gabriel eases up and moves his hand to hold Darrek by the base of his scrotum. The release of pressure on his testicles draws a heavy exhale from Darrek that's followed quickly by a keening sound as Gabriel uses his free hand to knead the sensitive organ, rolling Darrek's balls against his other hand. A few dribbles of fluid pulse from Darrek's slit and he gapes, head thrown back, mouth fallen open wide.

"It's okay. I'm not going anywhere yet," Gabriel hushes. "Can I let go?"

Darrek gulps down a breath and rolls his hips, his erection bobbing, a dark purplish red, the tip covered now in a film of shining fluid.

"When we come back here later," Gabriel tells him quietly. "How about I hogtie you, dip your balls in mouthwash and work a thick plug inside your ass. Maybe I'll even fuck you with it for a while, if you're good. How's that sound?"

Darrek growls and pants. His eyes bore sharply into Gabriel, hidden behind fallen, sun-kissed hair. "Promise?" he asks.

"I promise," Gabriel swears. "Should I let you come?"

"No," Darrek growls.

"Good. 'Cause I wasn't going to anyway."

He lets go of Darrek for a second and caresses tenderly over his slave's aching erection. It seems to aggravate Darrek even more than the pain had, so Gabriel steadies him in one hand and slaps his cock twice, back-and-forth, before releasing him for the last time as Darrek whimpers softly but appears peaceful.

Gabriel leaves him only to retrieve the aforementioned plug. Holding his legs in position, drawn up and apart, Darrek exhales a long moan as Gabriel fills him with the toy, nestling it snugly.

"Feel good?"

"Yes," Darrek gushes urgently. "Thank you, Master."

Gabriel slips the pink suit up Darrek's legs and helps him adjust himself to get into it. Once that impossible task is managed, Gabriel kisses Darrek's lips softly and murmurs, "I adore you. You're magnificent."

The trip to the beach lasts about an hour. Wearing a pair of big, wraparound sunglasses, Darrek is able to hide some of his bashfulness from onlookers as Gabriel leads him by the hand to a cabana. Moving more stiffly than usual due to his arousal and the plug, Darrek draws the attention of men and women alike. They stare unabashedly at him and even murmur their praise to Gabriel as they pass. Once they arrive at the cabana, Gabriel takes a seat, watching protectively over Darrek, lounging on a recliner on his stomach. Quickly, a waiter arrives to take their drink orders. The breeze off the ocean is brisk and refreshing, the sun warm, the sky cloudless. It seems the entire island is out on the sand, it's so packed with people.

Every stranger nearby can't help but stare, and every lingering or sneaked glance is a triumph for Gabriel. Darrek stays quiet, impossibly beautiful in Gabriel's eyes as well as everyone else's.

The highlight of the morning is when, in a fit of exhibitionism, Gabriel decides to fuck Darrek's mouth right there in the cabana on the white sands of the beach, mere feet from the crystal blue waters. Turning his back to the crowd, giving Darrek all of his attention, he takes each pigtail in hand and uses them as handholds as he rides his slave's mouth.

From where he's kneeling in the soft, warm sand, Darrek notices plenty of onlookers gathering around to watch. Gabriel pays them no mind, so Darrek tries to do likewise. It's difficult, though. They're all *right there,* with nothing besides Gabriel's back blocking their view as the cock slides in and out between his wet, stretched lips. That alone would be a lot to handle, but the added stress of the outfit, the makeup, and the hairdo, along with all of the conflicted feelings created by them, add up rapidly. Heart pounding, feeling more self-conscious than he remembers ever being in the whole of his life, Darrek closes his eyes.

He can still feel their eyes like fingers on him, skittering over his skin, noticing every detail. Tuning them out as best he can, he leaves Gabriel in absolute control and tries to revel in the freedom of total abandon. Knowing none of the people nearby can speak to him, touch him, or even get close, helps Darrek to feel safe. He reminds himself, too, of how they wouldn't be watching if they weren't compelled to do so by their own desire. In a way, it's empowering to know he's captivated so many people by dressing and behaving the way he is.

Gabriel yanks on Darrek's hair, twisted up on either side of his head, as he pulls Darrek's mouth forward to take the next thrust. Darrek is careful to keep his hands behind his back and out of the way, trusting in his Master to know what his tolerance level is and what he can handle. Sliding inward and slipping back out at a steady, measured pace, Gabriel is more careful than he is typically.

While Darrek struggles with his own boundaries, skating the edge, he can simultaneously tell how much Gabriel is enjoying being watched, sharing their pleasure with anyone who wants to look. He's getting off on it, marking Darrek, again, as his own, *his* property, knowing that no one else can have him like this. When he thinks about it that way, it's a power rush, intoxicatingly rich.

Once Gabriel climaxes, and Darrek has swallowed every drop, Gabriel discreetly tucks himself back into his suit without flashing the rest of the beach and everyone staring avidly at them. Other couples have taken their cues from them and begun to play with each other as well, but Gabriel doesn't appear to care. He helps Darrek wipe his mouth, nose and eyes dry, using a spare towel to clean him up, then orders another drink for them both. In that moment, Darrek feels joyful, sated, and grateful. It was the right decision to trust Gabriel's judgment, and push himself in a new way. Even though he was scared, it paid off and he's left feeling even stronger than he was before for having conquered another fear. His happiness is only amplified when he realizes the same emotions and understanding are being reflected back at him through Gabriel's gorgeous grayish-blue eyes.

A few days later, Gabriel agrees to wear a duplicate of the ridiculous pink bathing suit he'd dressed Darrek in. Darrek's anticipation makes him giddy as the promise of payback draws near. While Gabriel gets ready in the bathroom, as Darrek affords him the privacy he wasn't granted, Darrek waits impatiently by the bed.

As much as he might pretend to resent Gabriel's testing of Darrek's limits, truly, Darrek would never have it any other way. The more Gabriel dares his lover to find even more reserves of inner strength and bravery, the more Darrek is shocked by his own ability to meet the most daunting of challenges. Plus, Darrek loves to see Gabriel light up during their scenes, transforming into the spectacular Dominant Darrek first fell in love with.

That night, however, it's not the Dominant whom Darrek wants to enjoy, but Gabriel's irresistibly sweet, vulnerable side.

When Gabriel emerges from the bathroom, dressed in the miniscule, form-fitting, nearly obscene hot pink suit, his skin dusted with sparkling powder, Darrek has only a fraction of a second before his knees go weak and he's at Gabriel's feet. Clasping Gabriel's legs, dragging open-mouthed kisses over the velvety soft, warm skin of his exposed hip and navel, Darrek doesn't even try to hold in his moans. Maybe it's his imagination, but Gabriel even seems to *taste* sweeter as Darrek mouths down to the bulge in the suit's front.

Sighing heavily with his own pleasure, Gabriel takes hold of Darrek's hair again, as he had on the beach, lacing his fingers through the strands and massaging Darrek's scalp.

"Like it?" Gabriel asks. He smiles coyly even as his brow furrows with want. "I can be your girl for a little while...."

Darrek's only reply is a harder moan.

In a swift movement, he gets to his feet, sweeping Gabriel up in his arms and carrying him to bed.

A few days earlier, for *hours* Darrek had remained dolled up, turned on, and reveled in the highs of orgasm denial for Gabriel's amusement. All the while, he'd fantasized about how he was going to make Gabriel pay when he wore his suit in public as well, and possibly take photographic evidence to enjoy privately later. But, when faced with the reality of beautiful Gabriel dressed like living candy Darrek could suck on all night, it changes all of Darrek's careful plans. Hearing Gabriel actually *say it*, how he's dressed as a woman only for Darrek's pleasure, something Darrek suspects Gabriel has never done before with anyone else, it flips a switch inside him. There's no holding back, or drawing out the moment. Darrek's secret need for exactly what Gabriel is offering him is too great. As someone who's attracted to both men and women, it's one of the biggest turn-ons Darrek has ever experienced to have the man he loves playing the part of Darrek's girl, if only for a little while.

Gabriel doesn't wind up wearing his suit for very long at all. The more Gabriel tries to somehow look macho as his bulge threatens to burst the miniscule suit at the seams, his firm butt cheeks only half concealed by the shimmery, slick fabric, Darrek is forced to give it up. Forget the smidgeon of revenge. Forget even the camera; all he wants is to get his hands on his prize — the wonderful man who he's been lucky enough to belong to for two glorious years, and hopefully many, many more to come.

If you enjoyed this story, you can sign up for a free membership at
ForbiddenFiction and discuss it with other readers
and the author at the *Pleasures of Paradise* story page at
http://forbiddenfiction.com/library/story/LK1-1.000215.

Escape

Marriage, new names and a fresh start have helped Liam and Jacen Timothy leave their old lives behind. Now safer and deeply in love, Liam persuades Jacen to share part of his past he never has been able to before. Many years earlier, while recovering at his family's farm from his injuries, caring for his injured younger brother, Travis was unable to run when his predator, a neighbor, comes and seeks him out. Blackmail and threats move Travis to cooperate, for the sake of helpless, beloved Dennis. As Travis is consumed by a truly terrible, horribly familiar nightmare, it's his instincts and knack for survival against all odds that reveals to him, at long last, the way out. (M/M)

Escape

It was one of those rainy day mornings where the bed was too comfortable, too inviting. Liam Timothy lay warm and beautiful in his husband's arms and there was no good reason to get up just yet. Thunder rolled overhead. Gusts of wind blew rain against the windows. The farther Jacen Timothy burrowed into his pillow, the more Liam smiled. If that smile was meant to inspire Jacen to want to get up, it wasn't working. All it made him want to do was draw Liam down with him under the blankets. When he did, and Liam chuckled softly, Jacen realized maybe that had been the intention all along.

Liam rolled on top of him, arms winding closely around; his lips flush to Jacen's cheek. He could feel them curl in a smile against his skin. Liam's soft laughter reverberated through Jacen's body like more thunder and teeth scraped gently over the edge of Jacen's jaw. Growling softly, Jacen rolled them again. As he gaze down at his beloved, he saw the flash as Liam's diamond chip dermal piercing caught the room's dim light, refracting it in rainbows of color. The glimmer of true happiness and the glow of comfort shone in his gorgeous green eyes.

"Mmm," Jacen hummed, surrendering as Liam drew him down once more. Fingers wove through the strands of Jacen's long hair. A slim, muscular leg slung over the backs of his thighs. "You smell nice."

There was a passing glimpse of something undeniable in Liam's expression. He pulled Jacen in even tighter; their bodies flush together, and kissed beside Jacen's left eye. The silken touch of Liam's lips held there, that spark of burning determination alight. Jacen could feel it infusing Liam's body as his spirit strengthened his will. When

Jacen's husband wanted something, he was likely to get it. This was all part of the seduction, softening Jacen up before the request was voiced. Luckily, there was nothing Jacen enjoyed more than being seduced by Liam.

"What?" Jacen ventured, captivated by the golden curl of Liam's eyelashes.

Nuzzling against his husband's neck, Liam said quietly, "Tell me about it? When you left Travis behind? You promised you would."

Even just the mention made Jacen want to writhe.

Ghosts of memory wound around him, but Liam held him tighter, soothing with caresses along the muscles of Jacen's back when they tensed as if bracing for pain, murmuring a loving, "It's okay."

Jacen had never been so loved, so cherished as he was with Liam. Astonishingly, that affection did make it easier to dare to remember, revisiting a part of his former life he never intended to unearth again.

"It's not a pretty story," Jacen warned. His fingers grasped at Liam's shoulder and carded through soft blond hair. The natural scent of Liam filled Jacen's head, so intangible but somehow, wonderfully, more powerful than the old fears. Liam was there with him. The rest—everything he had been afraid of—was gone. It had been gone for years.

"Pretty? Like my story?" Liam asked. There was that eerie echo of Avery in the words, beneath the layers built on top of the child that was, that lost little boy, in search of love and home, grown into the incredible man who had bound himself and his fate to Jacen's, for better or worse.

A shiver raced up Jacen's back, part of the old fear, but Liam felt it there, and kissed it away, replacing hurt with hopeful caring with the skill of one who has learned, through trial and effort, the craft of healing. Wrapped up in Liam, Jacen was hidden inside the safety of their home, surrounded by loved ones, in a place of serenity which together they earned through their efforts to break free of old identities, and the chains of prostitution and helplessness. Jacen had earned that, had fought for it with everything that was in him. With blood and sex, pain and lust, terror and faith, he had followed the path he had set for himself, long ago, and, miraculously, had wound up where he was.

He was happy. He was blessed. Most of all, he was lucky.

"You have enough pain in here," Jacen sighed, laying a hand on Liam's chest, over his heart, feeling it bump against his palm. "I don't want to make you carry mine too."

"I love you," Liam said to him. "You believe that, right? And you love me even though I was a whore and a liar, and even though I buried Tim. Do you love me less for knowing about Timothy? Look at where we are. Think of what we have now. We're married. You're stuck with me. So tell me. Please, baby."

"It's terrible," Jacen warned, hissing the words, needing Liam to realize what he was asking.

"Maybe," Liam allowed. "But you're beautiful, and strong, and we already know your story has a happy ending."

He snuck a glance at Liam's face, seeing him bite at the edge of his lip, one eyebrow raised.

"God," Jacen groaned. "I can't tell if that sounds dirty or arrogant."

Liam burst into laughter. Infectious, it caught Jacen too.

"Please, baby," Liam pleaded so gently. "Share this with me. You'll feel lighter. Promise."

Thinking that if anyone would understand, it would be this man who loves Jacen so much, he sighed in surrender and murmured, "Okay."

For two months, Travis Saxon, a man grown and at long last an adult by rights, had foreseen the inevitable return of his childhood demon. Once discharged from the hospital with two leg casts—one partial, one full, he knew it was only a matter of time before Brian Andrews would seek him out. Mr. Andrews had preyed upon Travis since his age could be tallied in single digits. He had endured over ten years of rape and terror, and Travis had thus far told absolutely no one about it in order to protect the family he loved so dearly. The abuse had always ebbed and flowed like the tides. It could be spread thin, barely distinguishable, or flooding in a torrent. As Travis had been away at college for over a year, it had been a long while since the last episode.

It was overdue.

Travis's parents had taken his siblings — all of them but Dennis — into town to shop for supplies for Sunday supper. Travis and Dennis, both victims of the Thanksgiving Day car accident that had broken Travis's body and Dennis's mind, had been left behind to mind the house on the family's dairy farm. Dennis was the driver during the accident, and the proud new owner of the truck that was totalled after a drunk ran them off the road. Now all Dennis cared about was the cartoon playing on the television in the den and the pain that riddled his body as his physical wounds slowly healed. Painkillers helped as the bones knitted back together and the bruises gradually faded, but nothing could help the fact that Travis's beloved little brother was lost to them, never to return. The head trauma was simply too great for hope of any real recovery.

A small party had been planned for that early-winter evening to celebrate Travis's coming home, but home was the last place he wanted to be. College had been a major victory, his escape, his ticket out of town and away from the man that had made his torment a personal project for most of his life. Now that the college fund which had given him an escape route out of his private enslavement was suddenly gone, spent on astronomical medical bills, Travis was back in Hell, with any dream of salvation destroyed like the strength in his legs, and his sweet little brother's connection to the world. Misery and grief were things Travis had struggled with during the entirety of his hospital stay as the truth sank in, so in a twisted sort of way, it was a relief to see Mr. Andrews walking up the path to the back door.

A few years older than Travis's father, Brian Andrews, whose farmstead was less than a quarter-mile away, looked his age and then some, with grey hair and a thin, pinched face. He had a large nose and a farmer's build. Tall and physically strong, with rough hands and deceptively warm brown eyes, he appeared at first glance to be rather unassuming and average. With a reserved, polite demeanor, the adults that knew Mr. Andrews didn't think much of him, other than with admiration for his work ethic. The local children who knew him appreciated the in-ground pool on his property and the open invitation to swim there on hot summer days. He always had a hand-carved cane in hand, when he was walking around his property or coming for a visit at the Saxon household.

It was the sight of this very cane that made Travis's heart leap up into his throat and skin crawl with goosebumps as Mr. Andrews opened the screen door and stepped inside without a knock or a word. Good neighbors like him didn't need to give warning or wait to be invited in, according to Mr. and Mrs. Saxon. A shrewd observer might have noticed that Mr. Andrews didn't lean on the dark, polished wooden staff clutched in his hand at all as it tapped against the floorboards. Everyone but Travis wrote the cane off as a quirk or a comfort object for the old farmer. But Travis knew the truth. Yes, he certainly did. He felt physical echoes of that very truth as his own personal devil smiled in triumph and crossed the room. A weathered, tough right hand gripped the gently curved handle, almost caressing the smooth lacquer of the finish.

With his fingers hooked around his wheelchair's rims, the pain from the multiple breaks in his legs a constant, ceaseless throb, Travis didn't feel the teardrops as they began to fall from his jaw to his dampen his shirt after coursing their way around his nose and lips, and over his cheeks. Sniffling quietly, he stared out at nothing, and was nothing but unmoving and unspeaking. The clamor was all inside. *Boom-boom-boom-boom* went his heartbeat as the cheerful noise from the cartoon played in tinny softness from the next room where Dennis was propped up in a rented hospital bed.

"Hey there. I saw your folks drive past," Mr. Andrews said pleasantly, glancing into the den. "Let's go for a walk."

"Please don't." It was a warbled and raspy pathetic whisper of a plea. Travis always felt the same age in those moments. He would always be eight. For the rest of his life, a part of him would always be stuck right there, trying to get out and failing. "Leave me alone."

"Oh, you're busy? I'll just ask Dennis to join me, then." Mr. Andrews raised his eyebrows in question, not a drop of malice visible in his long face or tone of voice as he pointed over a shoulder to the broken, helpless form of seventeen-year-old Dennis Saxon. Dennis, who looked so very much like Travis, but younger, smaller, and utterly unable to understand what had happened to him to earn him such confusion and suffering; who he was, where he was, or what evil might befall him next. "You sit tight. I'll have him back in an hour."

Mr. Andrews's hand rubbed down over the curve in the handle of his cane and Travis moaned. The sound of it carried, disturbingly loud in the stillness, but it wouldn't be held in. The darkness opened below Travis, and he started to fall, just tumbling, tumbling down. Two more teardrops fell onto his collarbone and Travis heard himself say, from somewhere up above, where the cold light of day was coming in through the window over the sink, making the air sparkle with minuscule particles of dust, "You don't touch him. You don't *ever*—"

The cane swung in a wide arc, falling with a snap against Travis's shin beside where the pins held his tibia together.

He couldn't even scream. If he screamed, he would upset Dennis and there would be no calming him down until their mother got home, so Travis swallowed his agony as best he could, with sobs and gasps and a shrill keening.

"I'm sorry, I didn't catch that, Travis?" Mr. Andrews cupped a hand to his ear, leaning forward slightly. "Do you know what would really be a shame? If you were to roll over to the door there, leading to the basement, and fall right down the steps. Why, I bet you'd re-break those legs of yours! You might break your neck, too. That'd be a real shame, wouldn't it? Why don't I roll you safely away from there, huh? You bet!"

Travis said nothing as Mr. Andrews took the wheelchair by its handles and pushed him toward the back door, where his father had only last week built a ramp leading to the driveway for him to use. They left the house, and Mr. Andrews made sure that the door was closed securely behind them. The walk down the drive and up the road to the Andrews' farm, though sunny, frigid and cloudless, was a tepid, dense, grey fog for Travis. Far above where his body existed, apart from his consciousness, he hovered, hearing the voice of his nightmares tell him how wonderful it was that Travis broke his legs, so that he had to come home, and couldn't run away anymore. But Travis knew that it wasn't real; it was only the nightmare again and went back to the fog, where it was safer and the boogeyman couldn't find him.

The chair tipped back as Mr. Andrews got Travis up onto the back patio and then rolled him into the house. As Travis had known for over a decade, there was a guest room at the back of the Andrews farmhouse, through the downstairs washroom and behind a solid oak door. There were special notches both inside and outside of the doorframe that no one had ever seen in use, except for Travis and Mr. Andrews. That was where the bolts went to make sure no one got out, or in.

Past the washroom, through the doorway, Travis was tipped violently forward. Falling out of the chair, trying to brace his fall with his arm, he saw the brutal agony he was about to feel but knew he wouldn't be able to stop it. His right leg in its full cast stuck awkwardly out, straight out in front of him, and was directly in the way. That hit the bed first and then he did scream as he landed face-down. The pain was intense enough to turn the grey fog an inky black. Sounds receded farther — like the click of the bolt after the whoosh of the door closing. The only sensation Travis was aware of was the torture of his shattered, pinned-together legs slamming against the mattress, especially in his right upper thigh. He didn't notice at all when his shirt was pushed up, his pants opened, and yanked down along with his underwear to the top of the cast. Even when the heavily lacquered wood of the cane's handle was forced through his sphincter and into his rectum, dry, lodged deeply in the delicate tissues, it only registered on a base level, so familiar it didn't merit additional alarm at all. It was left in there, with the length of the cane lying up against Travis's back as the touching started, and the recitation of old promises.

"I want your smell on there. I keep sniffing the handle, and it makes me sad when it doesn't smell like you. You don't want me to be sad, do you, Travis?"

The throbbing in his rectum was nothing to him, and easily ignored. For Travis the only true worry, even when his legs were pushed apart widely and the old man started sucking and slobbering between them, burying his face in there, was whether, even if he was very quiet and very still, Mr. Andrews would hurt his legs anymore. They hurt so much. Unsurprisingly to either of them, no matter how Mr. Andrews used his mouth or tongue on him, Travis remained flaccid. The attention wasn't for Travis' benefit anyway, though it did make it more difficult for Travis to fold himself up in the fog when the black slipped through his fingers, no matter how fervently he grasped for it.

He just wanted it to be over. He didn't fight, or protest, or move, and only lay prone, breathing, glassy-eyed, and with a vacant stare. Like always, he would have remained that way except an engine sounded somewhere nearby, vibrating in his ear. Horribly, aware-ness—total and clear—gripped him as he tried to figure out where the sound came from. If it was his parents returning early from their errands, that indicated many problems—only one of them being that Dennis had been left all alone. If, instead, it was someone from Mr. Andrews's family—his wife or children, perhaps—that would be bad for Travis in a different way. It would quickly become necessary to keep him quiet and well-behaved and that would only mean bond-age and more pain. Thankfully, it was only a plane passing by low overhead.

The fog was completely gone, though, leaving him hyperaware of the clench of his buttocks around the cane's grip, the thickness of the handle stretching him out and filling him up. The slimy tongue snaked its way over his testicles and up the underside of his penis before it pulled away. Mr. Andrews noticed Travis's state of alert.

"You like that, huh? Yeah, you do," Mr. Andrews said. The tongue dragged wetly over the curve of his left buttock and fingers pulled the muscle, spreading him. When fingers rubbed over his rim, around where the wood entered him, Travis groaned thickly and wrapped his arms over his head to block it out. The groan became a heavy grunt when the cane was tugged back out only to push back in along with a couple of licked fingers. Mr. Andrews had to use more force and work at the outer ring of muscle to manage it, licking there to lubricate.

Once the fingers were in him, along with the cane, that particu-lar intimate ache won out over the wild riot in his legs. Travis cried out with thick, unbidden sounds. "What do we say, Travis?" he was asked.

"Thank you," he choked out.

"Do you like it?"

The handle and fingers pumped steadily, and he controlled the urge to flinch or show how much it hurt.

"Yes, Mr. Andrews."

"Is there something you want instead?"

Travis detached, looking for the fog. When he found it right where he had left it, he pushed his mind into it, getting lost there. He relaxed slightly, some of the tension leaving his tortured body as he discovered solace and, somewhere far away, recited the practiced lines like an old pro.

"I want your cock. Please fuck me."

"Now, Travis, I really shouldn't do something like that. What would your family say?"

"They'll never find out. I promise."

The fingers pulled the curved handle out, leaving him stretched and sore. The old man moved around him, getting between Travis's legs. He climbed on after his pants were pulled down, but of this, Travis had no idea until the old farmer's closed fist punched down on the back of Travis's right upper thigh.

Pain.

So much pain, and nothing had ever hurt like it, not with everything that Mr. Andrews had ever done to him. It woke Travis again, denying him any comfort from his old coping mechanisms. Past shrieking, unable to inhale oxygen around the tidal wave of pain like a red-hot metal spike driven through his femur as it grew and grew and grew, the urge to retch was strong and for a second he did gag, but controlled the reflex with the skill of a survivor.

"You know I like when you put up a fight for me. Makes you almost as tight as you were when we first met."

In a dull way, Travis did feel the rhythmic pumping into his body, but it didn't reach him, and he didn't care, really. Agony was exponentially worse than the fucking. It was better to give Mr. Andrews what he wanted to avoid punishment. He put up a lame attempt at fighting back, and it was an adequate distraction anyhow. Time passed and only after a remarkably long while did Travis become fully aware of himself and of being untouched.

It was quiet.

Glancing around, Travis saw that the door was unbolted and closed. He was alone with the wetness leaking down his inner thigh. The wheelchair was almost near enough to grab. It took him long, long minutes of effort to get his pants back up and the chair rolled over to the edge of the bed, so that he could scramble backward into the seat of his chair.

Before he could roll to the bedroom door—though he wanted to, very much—he noticed a small, empty disc case beside the camera. The camera was always there, but discs and cases never were. It had been a while, he thought. Maybe old age and being out of practice had made Mr. Andrews sloppy. Travis frantically pushed himself over to the bureau, turning the wheels with his hands, and opened the camera's tray. The disc was there, and he stared at it without moving to take it. Then he closed the camera, leaving it as it was. A small television with a DVD player sat there as well, like it always had, and inspiration struck. On a whim, praying harder than he had since he was eight, Travis checked the topmost drawer. Discs were scattered inside, like they had been recently watched and had yet to be put away. They were unmarked other than with a small date written in black ballpoint pen on the label. The date on the solitary disc he selected and scooped up was from ten years ago.

A huge, elated smile broke across Travis's face. Clutching the tiny disc to his chest, he almost laughed.

"Thank you, God. Oh, thank you, God. Thank you."

He secreted the precious treasure away into a pocket in the side of the wheelchair, and knew exactly what he needed to do. It was not about him anymore, it was about Dennis. If Dennis, guilty of nothing but being a naïve teenage boy who thought no real harm could ever befall him, could be made to give up everything but his life by fate and God, then Travis could try to be just as brave. He would give it up—all of it. He would sacrifice his loved ones, his home, his pride, his secrets, and his future. The only thing he would get in return was away. Thinking of Dennis, thinking of elusive vengeance, too, he decided that getting away, and staying alive, was plenty.

Undisturbed as he exited the bedroom and left the Andrews residence—Mr. Andrews had always left escape up to Travis to manage, or stay if he preferred—Travis used all of the strength in his arms, thinking of things like rehab, the names of local television stations, the number for the local police office, phone calls to be made and the newfound hard evidence which might at long last save him when no one and nothing else could.

Jacen was lost there, years in the past. He was Travis again and the scream was so close, rising in his throat. He pushed at the hands holding him, fighting back, fresh tears dampening his cheeks, blurring his vision.

Liam's voice, strong, clear and true, pierced the fog. "Hey. Baby. Jacen. *Jacen.*"

There was patience, tenderness and understanding. He heard it, and grasped for them, knowing they were his lifeline, his rescue. He met Liam's eyes, which were searching so fiercely for Jacen, whose was face held tenderly in Liam's hands. Liam said, "I see you. I hear you. You're okay. You're home. You're *home.*"

Liam moved into Jacen's open arms, holding Jacen as Jacen gripped Liam tightly, letting out a shaky exhale tinged with a low moan filled with hurt.

"He can't hurt you anymore," Liam swore. "You made sure of that. You were so brave."

When Jacen responded, his voice sounded strange to his own ears, drifting somewhere between the identities of Jacen and Travis. "The worst part had nothing to do with physical pain. It was the *waiting.* Worse than whenever I was waiting for him to come find me again, was waiting for all of those people to react to the footage of him raping me, for the news to come out and my family to hear. I didn't know what would happen to Mr. Andrews and I couldn't do anything about it. And I didn't know how to hope that it would turn out okay."

"You were afraid because you couldn't be there to protect Dennis. God, you must have been so scared," Liam sighed. He pulled back a little to better search Jacen's eyes. "You okay?"

Jacen drew in the scent of him. Everything that was good, everything that helped Jacen accept that it had been worth it, was wrapped up in the warmth of Liam's skin. Because Jacen would never have found Liam if not for everything he had endured during his childhood and adolescence, and everything Liam had also endured in his. Their paths had come together, and merged. Who knows where they would be, otherwise?

"Yeah," Jacen murmured, nodding. He took a deep breath and slowly let it out. "They found more evidence when they searched Mr. Andrews' place. Then he was arrested. It was over and I just had to figure out where to go from there. Feels like such a long time ago."

"Proud of you," Liam whispered urgently, frowning and pressing a kiss to the center of Jacen's brow.

"Proud of you too," Jacen replied.

Everything was quiet. The rain had stopped. The thunder had cleared. The room itself was brighter as the sun broke through the clouds above.

"Let's go for a walk, okay?" Liam suggested. "We can take the dogs? Fresh air?"

"Yeah," Jacen agreed, smiling a little.

A few minutes later, Jacen had the dogs—a pair of mastiffs belonging to their friend and landlord—on their leashes and watched as they played, jumping around. Liam always took longer to get ready, so Jacen waited outside for him to lock up the house. When he finally appeared, Jacen began to laugh helplessly, the rest of the tension in him melting away at the sight of his husband dressed in a nice pair of tailored pants, a crisp, black-and-grey-striped button down shirt with hardly any buttons closed, and wearing a cocky little hat tilted to one side.

"You're not wearing a fedora," Jacen beamed, loving Liam so much in that moment that it made him dizzy.

"Oh, I absolutely am," Liam grinned, tugging on the brim and angling it even more.

"Since when do you even have one?" Jacen asked, still laughing and shaking his head with amazement.

"Never underestimate the contents of my closet."

"Oh, I don't," Jacen assured him. The dogs were hopping with excitement and circling around Liam. While Jacen worked to untangle them, the leashes only drew Jacen and Liam closer and closer together. Looping an arm around Liam's waist, kissing him full on the lips, Jacen said, "You look adorable."

"Of course I do!" Liam grinned, so handsome he stole Jacen's breath away.

"I love you so much," Jacen told him, speaking directly from the heart. It was the truth which guided him now. "You're amazing, Mr. Timothy."

Slinging an arm behind Jacen's neck after almost falling over one of the dogs, Liam kissed him back and replied, "No, *you're* amazing, Mr. Timothy."

All around them, the world was greener and more lush from the rain. Sunbeams shone down from overhead as the storm clouds blew away, replaced by clear blue sky. The world was reflected in tiny mirrors made by puddles on every surface around them. The dogs raced away toward the gate, ready for adventure, Liam held Jacen's hand, and Jacen knew it was going to be a very good day.

Trick and Truth

Avery Williams needs to be someone else. Anyone else would be an escape from the harsh reality facing him. Tonight, that someone is Jimmy, his roommate, who goes dancing at the gay clubs in the city. As Jimmy, Avery finds what he needs — sex with a stranger who pays handsomely for the privilege. But once the fantasy has ended, all that's left is the painful, unavoidable truth waiting at home. (M/M)

Trick and Truth

It isn't a decision at all, but a solution; the difference between the two, night and day. That's what Avery Williams tells himself. Choice versus answer, and the answer—as damning as it is—has been staring him in the face all along.

The idea comes from one of Avery's housemates, Jimmy. Jimmy's actual name is Patrick O'Donnell. Like everyone else in their circle of friends/former-foster-siblings, now all recently aged out of the system, Patrick was given a nickname to christen his new life. The obvious ones came first; his name was shortened to Paddy, but, over time, became Irish, which shifted to Jameson, and finally settled on Jimmy (chosen in honor of a certain knack for picking locks).

Jimmy, formerly Patrick, is a thin, short, freckled young man with an obsession for clubbing. When Jimmy goes out, he goes *all* out, dressing flamboyantly, dancing until he can barely stand, and hooking up with whoever suits his needs. In the process, he always has the time of his life. He acts his age, and for a while feels like a normal teenager rather than a poverty-stricken throwaway who is barely managing to stay off of the streets. It's the perfect role to play, Avery thinks, intending to borrow Jimmy's persona for his own benefit. Avery is tired of being himself anyway. This is a chance for him to also pretend to be simply wild, free and young for a few precious hours.

By the time Avery applies some of Jimmy's gold glitter make-up around the outsides of his green eyes, down his pronounced cheekbones, and over his chest, and puts on what on any other day would be for him a ridiculous outfit—also Jimmy's—of yellow short shorts and a white, fitted tank top, Avery is already mentally—if not physically—at the club, and not at all in the run-down building they call home. Up-tempo, bass-heavy music plays loudly in his headphones, rattling his brain, drowning out the sound of the nightmare waiting at the back of the house and the painful, hacking coughs from the bedroom there. That's where Timothy is, Avery's boyfriend, another former-foster-brother turned somehow into the love of Avery's life. When Avery puts on a pair of Jimmy's gold-tinted, white-framed glasses, the peeling wallpaper and cracked plaster of the walls seem instantly less dreary. There's only one more thing he needs, and then he can leave. Skin crawling with an overwhelming desire to bolt from the place, stomach churning with a queasy, adrenaline-fueled sort of anticipation, Avery crosses from the bathroom they all share to a closed door near the flight of stairs leading to the first floor and the exit. Three raps of his knuckles on the discolored wood and the door swings open.

Jimmy's reaction to Avery's transformation from shy, skinny gutter-rat to barely-dressed club kid is complicated, though largely unnoticed as Avery tunes it all out anyway. If he *did* have any interest in his friend and foster-brother's opinion, Avery would find Jimmy to first be surprised, then amused, and finally, all the amusement withers, rotting on Jimmy's face once he sees the haunted emptiness in Avery's young eyes. Behind the foolish gold glasses, making everything look sunshiny and bright, Avery is past horror, past screaming and furious hysteria, past even acceptance and profound grief. Nothing is left but stony resignation. It hurts Jimmy's heart to witness.

"Nice outfit, Pigeon," Jimmy says, using Avery's nickname, given for Avery's tendency to be hard to pin down, and his constant, shifting hunger for things like food, acceptance, love and life.

"Thanks," Avery mutters. His hand comes up to scratch restlessly and slightly self-consciously at a spot on his bare upper arm. "Can I borrow your boots? The white ones?"

"They won't fit you. Those shorts don't exactly fit you either." Avery is almost a foot taller than Jimmy. Much less of him is covered by the miniscule article of clothing.

"I'll make do. Promise I'll take care of them. Scout's honor."

"When were you ever a boy scout?" Avery glances impatiently towards the stairs, and isn't really listening anyway, so Jimmy sighs and relents. "One sec. They're around here somewhere."

In truth, Jimmy knows right where the knee-high leather boots are that he stole from the back of a Jag a few years ago. But he uses the few seconds that the feigned search buys him to try to think of something useful to say, or some argument to pose that won't lose him a brother or buy him a left hook. He comes up both empty-handed and not. Holding out the boots to Avery, but with nothing persuasive to say, Jimmy says, "Let me come with. It'll be a blast."

"No."

"Pidge, don't do this," Jimmy starts, wanting to kick the wall and yell in Avery's maddeningly impassive, pretty face.

The headphones have been pulled away from one of Avery's ears to allow him to hear his brother, but it also lets him hear other things. Another violent coughing fit erupts from the end of the hall and the sound of it tightens Avery's mouth. Gritting his teeth, frowning subtly, he suddenly looks forty instead of nineteen, with worry and wear taking its toll in spades, hollowing his handsome features, deadening his once-vibrant spirit.

"Gimme the fucking things," Avery snaps, yanking the boots from Jimmy and storming off to the staircase.

"Think about what you're doing, you stupid asshole! Think of Timothy," Jimmy rages, pouring all of his frustration and sorrow into the words, his pale skin heating instantly to a deep pink under countless freckles. Avery takes the steps two and three at a time, pushing the headphones back onto his ears, denying Jimmy's argument and rational logic. His choice is made. There's nothing left to do and words mean nothing.

The walk out of Camden, New Jersey, across the bridge spanning the river, and into Philadelphia is a long one. Avery had wrapped his feet tightly before cramming them into the too-small boots, but the seemingly endless miles cause blisters to quickly sprout on his feet nonetheless. It doesn't faze him, or slow him down. With long strides he chases the city, bigger than his own, and filled with more promise. Every stride takes him farther from his problems, farther from his beloved makeshift family and the truth. The night is warm, and he's glad for it, as skimpily dressed as he is. A few cars honk at him as they pass, and he turns each time, wondering if he won't have to walk all the way to the club after all. No one actually stops, though, so he continues on.

By the time he arrives at his destination and gets past the bouncer, he's nearly dizzy with the pain in his feet. Laughing it off, or trying to, he tucks his shirt behind a decorative panel in the wall, preferring to go bare-chested and show as much skin as possible. Clad in only the shorts and the boots, Avery lets himself be pulled by the human current towards the dance floor. Colored lights swing, arc and pulse in the darkness as the DJ holds court in the popular downtown gay club. Body heat and smoke of many sorts both thickens and sweetens the air. House music thumps in his head, beating under his skin, in his bones and teeth. Shaking his naturally golden blond hair, bouncing to the rhythm of the bass, he's soon swallowed up. Men of all ages, sizes and sorts press in on all sides. Some are also bare-chested, some aren't.

He loses track of time. The songs change. He gets thirsty, but that need is weaker than the ravenous hunger, so he easily puts it aside. The dance goes on.

Then, he sees his mark—a dark-haired, broad-shouldered guy in a blue polo shirt who looks to be at least twenty-five. The thing that really catches Avery's attention, though, is the expensive-looking watch on the man's wrist. And his shoes. Avery hasn't had shoes that nice in all of his life. While being moved from bed-to-bed and family-to-family in the foster care system, he learned early on that you can tell a lot about a person by the quality of their shoes. And in this moment, nothing else matters to Avery Williams but the size of the price tag on this particular stranger's shoes. Not his looks or personality—just the money that must have been spent on something as unimportant as accessories.

Avery snakes over to the mark, and starts dancing right in front of him, grinding against the guy's crotch and smiling with what he hopes reads as alluring, charming enticement. Working his attractive face for all it's worth, flaunting his lean body—trimmed down by starvation and toned by a complete lack of funds for any transportation method other than walking—and shaking his firm, shapely ass, showed off nicely in the tiny shorts, Avery lures in his prey. When the mark responds, Avery is so happy that he laughs and slips readily into the man's arms as they wind around him. Hands skim greedily down over Avery's body. For a few minutes, it's just dancing, nothing more, but Avery does his best to react with evident pleasure to each groping touch, inviting more of the same. Avery's impatience increases exponentially when he catches a glimpse of the time on the watch that had gotten him over here in the first place. It's getting late—too late—and he needs to hurry this up.

Turning in the older man's arms to face him, Avery bites seductively at his lower lip, his big, startlingly intelligent, bright eyes half-lidded with both a multi-layered weariness and lust.

"Let's go somewhere more private," Avery hears, right by the shell of his ear, half-shouted over the din.

"It'll cost you," he teases.

"Yeah? How much?"

Heart racing, his hips moving in a smooth, dipping roll inside another's hands, dizzy and desperate, he answers with only a remarkably slight quiver to his deep-pitched voice—belying his youth and inexperience, "Depends on what you're after."

A thick thigh slips between Avery's legs. With a slow drag, the top of the muscle brushes against his crotch. When he feels a playful, but deliberate squeeze of his ass, Avery has his answer.

"A hundred," he says as his gaze skitters around the room, looking everywhere at once as the cold fingers of panic and trepidation claw briefly at his mind, making him want to cry or yell or run. The rough, electronic barking of the song suddenly sounds like coughing. He grasps more tightly on to the arms encircling him and the hands playing with his ass to ground himself to the fantasy. The fantasy is so much better than the alternative.

With a subtle nod and an incline of his head, the broad-shouldered, rich guy leads young Avery away.

They find a relatively secluded hallway with a few other couples lurking in the gloom, tangled and rubbing against each other.

"What's your name?"

Strong hands turn him around to face the wall and the unknown man presses up against Avery's body from behind. Lips touch softly to his neck. Quickly, Avery pulls a condom from his pocket, passing it back. He gazes to his right, down the shadowy hall and towards the glowing, undulating dance floor beyond, packed with the sweaty, glistening bodies of the forever young, careless and free. Planting his hands in front of him, fingers splayed, as his hips are drawn back and the yellow shorts are pushed down in back, Avery says without hesitation, "I'm Jimmy."

"Hi, Jimmy." It's said with a smile and a breathy chuckle. Pulse pounding in his ears, chest tight, lungs burning, nerves jangling, Avery feels fingers probe into his body which spreads readily, but all too quickly they are pulled out. A big hand claws at his hip, tilting his pelvis at more of an angle and then there's intense pressure and it hurts, but Avery knows it's only because he's still very nervous, and tense. After taking a deep inhale of the club's polluted air through his nose, blowing it back out through his mouth, he gasps as he's breached. His face grows hot, bile brought of shame rises in his throat but then he thinks of Jimmy. Lucky Jimmy. Jimmy wouldn't be scared of a hookup in the dark. It'd be no big deal, and nothing to get worked up over. He'd just laugh and enjoy the ride.

Lucky Jimmy.

A hand reaches around Avery's slim body to squeeze a handful of his cock through the shorts pulled tight and bunched around it. With a low moan, filling his head with music — brash, loud, pumping, defiant, and reckless — and only music, Avery is only aware of the push, the intimate fullness and the ache. It's a good ache. The mark's stiffened, sheathed member burrows inch-by-inch into him, with little pushes and pulls. It makes him feel taken, owned and claimed, and Avery doesn't hide that he likes it, even from himself. He's always liked the feeling of belonging to someone, no matter who it might be, or how it happens. After all, it's far, far better to belong than to be unwanted.

When he's stuffed full, his young, lithe body stuck obscenely on the end of a stranger's dick, he can't hold in his cries. Moaning sharply, letting the sound get washed away by the torrent of humanity around him, he writhes as a hand scrambles and claws its way inside Avery's white briefs. Fingers roll hungrily over his bare flesh, fondling him. Then, he's eased free of his pants for anyone to see and slowly stroked hard. For a second, he's convinced he won't be able to manage an erection, but his body proves him wrong, telling him that if it feels good, that's all that counts. Others are watching. Hyperaware of the dick fucking him up the ass and the kiss of the air on his exposed genitals, he feels very much displayed. He is the entertainment now. From over his back there's grunting and pushing, the old familiar tug and thrust. By chance the expensive wristwatch catches a beam of light which swings over them, making the glass face shine green for a moment. Green like money and money is everything. It's sex and love and life and death. With a shudder and a twitch from his possessor, Avery realizes that their dance is done. Or maybe not.

"Dance with me again, Jimmy," he hears, guided to stand upright, and away from the wall. The mark moves both of their hips, their bodies joined so intimately, in a slight, dipping figure-eight, and Avery moans at the shifting of the engorged flesh inside him. He's pulled back to lean against the other man's chest, broader than his own. Winding an arm up to hook around his dance-partner's neck, turning his head to the side to allow a better view down his body, he lets the mark watch his own fingers sliding up and down Avery's dark, swollen column, straining up between his narrow hips, the borrowed yellow shorts tight around Avery's upper thighs. Feeling the eyes of the onlookers who are no more than shapes in the dark, and somehow getting off on it, with rapid tugs and greedy stimulation, he climaxes, shooting semen in hot, messy streaks over his stomach. The orgasm's power leaves him panting and wrung-out. The mark withdraws, pulling free, leaving Avery open and feeling well-used. It's tempting to want to close his eyes and wait for a sense of steadiness to return, but he can't. A voice in his head tells him to get his money, and now.

Facing his customer, Avery doesn't even have to ask. Two folded bills are pushed into his hand before he can think to raise it beseechingly.

It's that easy.

"Keep the change. Your ass was worth it."

The mark kisses his cheek and gets quickly lost in the crowd. Avery stands there, staring at the two hundred dollar bills, amazed. The hope, happiness and pride are so strong and so acute he starts to tear up even as he laughs. He covers himself, pulling the shorts back up, and makes a tight, protective fist around the money. Just before he's able to sprint from the hallway, he notices that the on-lookers are still looking. One of them, no more than a grey, towering shadow, motions to him, glancing ravenously down Avery's sweaty, just-fucked body.

"Hey you. C'mere," someone beckons.

"How much for the ass?" asks another. "I've got a few bucks."

Before the disgust can catch up with him and make him come down hard from his high, Avery runs like he's being chased. On his way, he grabs the hidden shirt near the entrance. Pulling it on, he knows where he needs to be.

The jog back to New Jersey leaves Avery with bloody feet and a limp. First, he goes to the drug store, where he buys cough medicine, soup and tea. The cashier looks at him strangely due to the outfit, but he's got a shirt, and shoes, and cash, so it's good enough to close the transaction. The next stop is harder. A few more miles and down an alley, he finds the right door.

The long, lecherous look he gets when his knock is finally answered by a small, hunched, bald old man makes Avery fold his arms over his chest, wanting a shower more desperately than he ever has. The semen has dried in crusty streaks over his belly and he can still feel the fingers playing with him, crawling like worms over his skin.

"I got it. I have the cash," Avery says, glancing all around, everywhere at once. "You said seventy-five for the AIDS meds."

"Nah, two hundred."

"I don't fucking have two hundred, I have seventy-five!" Avery bellows. He shows the bills, exact change from the pharmacy. "Come on! Unless you're not good for it. I know somewhere else I can try. I don't do business with liars anyway."

He starts to walk away.

"Okay! Fine! I'm good for it."

Avery sighs, lips forming the words to an unspoken prayer of thanks before he turns back around.

The white boots are peeled off as soon as he's on the front porch of his house. Hissing curses, he unwinds the tape around his feet and hurriedly examines the damage done before limping inside and closing the door as quietly as he can. He opens the can of soup and pours it into a pot, turning the heat on low to warm it. Wiping his feet free of blood, and then drying them, he goes to find some socks from the make-shift clothesline stretched across the laundry room. With that, Avery hobbles upstairs with the paper bag full of pills and cough medicine, and a glass of water. The hallway has never been longer.

Too slowly the back bedroom gets closer. He would shower and get changed before going further and facing inescapable judgment, but there's no time, and it doesn't matter anyway. Not anymore.

Avery pushes the door open without knocking and half-hops inside, walking on the outer-edges of his sore, battered feet.

Without raising his head to look up at the figure on the bed, he walks over and shakes the pill boxes and bottles out of the paper bag and onto the nightstand beside where he sets the water. His fingers work rapidly, though trembling, getting one of each kind free and palming them.

"What is this?" he is asked as he holds out the medication on an opened hand.

"Take 'em. Come on. The faster you take 'em, the faster they can start to work."

"It's not gonna help."

Finally, Avery looks up, and when he does, he sees the person he loves most in the whole of the world, no more or less, only that—not the thin, brittle look of the twenty-year-old boy's sandy colored hair, or the unnaturally dull hue of his skin. He doesn't see the dark circles or the sores either. They're there, though, even if he denies them, fighting back with the foolish hope of youth and naiveté.

"Take 'em. Take 'em and you'll get better. You'll see," Avery says, with the first spark of light that he's shown in a long time. He almost smiles. "The doctor said you needed these, so I got them. You'll get better now."

Timothy laughs at him with a sneer, but it turns into another one of those unending, chest-rattling coughing fits.

"I'm not going to get *better*, Avery," Timothy rasps, when it passes—Timothy, who had promised to love Avery forever, and take care of him until they were old and had lived long, normal, boring lives together. "You don't get better from this. It's not the fucking *flu*."

"They said this would help," he insists, softer now, "And it will. It'll help."

Timothy stares at Avery, and it's never been clearer that the natural joy that has always been there in Avery's true love has been chewed away by a sickness with well-sharpened teeth. Ever quick to laughter, always brave and hopeful beyond good sense, determined to take care of his own, at whatever cost, Timothy has been the best and biggest gift of Avery's life. And he's dying. His face is riddled with the telltale signs of the virus that is slowly tearing him apart, making him angry at everything, including the one person in the world fighting tooth and nail, with blood, semen and pieces of his soul to save him, somehow.

Timothy sees — the body glitter, the crusty, sweaty tank top, the ravaged feet, the shame.

Softly, sounding nothing but scared for the first time in months, and not just resigned or bitter, Timothy asks, "Where'd you get the money, baby?"

With sudden strength, Timothy's hand shoots out and digs in the front pocket of the stupid yellow shorts, pulling out a hundred dollar bill. There's only one thing that would get Avery a hundred.

"You stole it, right? You stole the money," Timothy declares in that same, small, hushed, rattled voice, knowing full-well that Jimmy is the thief, not Avery. "You stole the money, right? To pay for the pills?"

"It was," Avery says, feeling lightheaded and nauseous, wanting to run again, until his feet are bloody stumps, just as long as he gets away. Far, far away. "It was a... uh, long walk from the pharmacy, so I'm going to get cleaned up, okay? Take these and get some rest. I'm making soup, and I have tea. That'll be good for your throat."

"Just tell me first. *Please*," Timothy begs. With widened eyes and that small, childlike voice, he holds tightly on to Avery's hand. "Just tell me the truth. You took the money off of some idiot with a wallet sticking out of his back pocket. Just be honest. Tell me. Tell me the truth. Tell me that you made a bad decision, but it's done now and you'll never steal again. Please. *Please*, baby. I love you so much. So much, Avery. And I know I don't say that enough, okay, but I'm saying it. Okay? And you would never... You wouldn't do anything to hurt me. Not like that. You're not that cruel. You'd never let some stranger put his hands on you for *this*. A few dollars and some fucking *soup*."

"It's not for the soup," Avery says, breathlessly, his eyes fluttering closed as the room tilts. "I need something to eat. Tim, let me go. Take your pills. You'll get better if you take the pills."

"Not until you answer me. Swear to me, on everything we have, on how much we love each other, on the good heart that I know you to have, that you did not fuck a stranger for *this*."

"I won't lose you," Avery gasps as the tears start to fall. There have been so many tears, he thought he'd run out. They blur his vision as he tries to pull free, but can't, because now he's the weak one. "Do you hear me?! I won't."

"You will. But I won't take you with me when I go. I WON'T!" Timothy shrieks. "I WON'T TAKE YOU AND I WON'T LEAVE YOU AS A FUCKING WHORE. My beautiful Avery..."

Avery breaks, sobbing. "Let go of me. *Let go of me*."

"No. I'll never let you go. You belong to me, not them. I'm the one that loves you! *I love you!*"

"You won't get to make the rules when you're dead," Avery snaps, his breath hitching, catching on the tears.

"I'm not dead yet." Timothy's mouth, once ever-smiling, and which Avery has kissed thousands, possibly millions of times, presses into a hard, thin, angry line. The best of him is gone, Avery thinks, closing his eyes against the sight to deny it. "Am I? *Am I!?*"

"No," Avery sighs, wincing.

"Why? Why would you, when you know... *you know* what this shit did to me? LOOK AT ME! Why? Baby, why? Is it because I've been mad? I won't be mad anymore, okay? I promise. It's the fucking virus. It's not me. You know it's not me. I need you to be safe. That's what I've always told you, isn't it? You need to be the one that's safe. It's my job to keep you *safe*."

"Okay," Avery nods, whining back in his throat, letting Timothy pull him down to sit on the edge of the bed and kiss his knuckles. But it's not enough, so Timothy draws Avery into a tight embrace, holding him protectively, smelling sweat, smelling blood and semen. "I stole the money. I won't do it again."

"Good," Timothy says, and smiles, but it's false and hides only heartbreak, pure and perfect. A whine of terror slips from behind his gritted teeth and he quickly bites it off. "That's good. I'll take the pills. You check the soup and then come back to lay with me, okay?"

"Okay," Avery nods, still crying, crying until he's nothing but a dry, hollow shell, but quietly now, as he passes Timothy the glass of water.

"You could get hurt stealing, you know," Timothy reminds him, latching on to the lie, looking infinitely more haggard and grey than even moments ago, when Avery first walked into the room, before Avery shattered Timothy's fragile hope that somehow, things might still be okay, even if he had to die. It wasn't bad enough that he lost his own life; now he's losing Avery too.

Timothy takes the glass and downs a couple of pills before reaching for more. "I won't have you doing that shit for me. If you love me, you won't ever do it again. Promise you won't."

"Okay, baby. I won't do it again. I promise. Cross my heart."

And it wasn't me anyway, Avery reminds himself. It was Jimmy all along.

If you enjoyed this story, you can sign up for a free membership at
ForbiddenFiction and discuss it with other readers
and the author at the *Trick and Truth* story page at
http://forbiddenfiction.com/library/story/LK1-1.000028.

Between Here and There

Ever the tease, Avery Williams leads his lover, Timothy, on a chase that brings them to Ben Franklin bridge spanning the Delaware River. Behind them is Camden and their daily struggle to stay off the streets. Before them is the vibrant, elusive promise of the future. Trapped between, Avery lets himself be caught by the boy who owns his heart. Dreams and demons alike lie in wait as Avery gives Timothy yet another piece of himself in the hopes that it will somehow save them both. (M/M)

Between Here and There

Far above the dark expanse of the Delaware River, Avery Williams leans over the bridge's thick metal railing, looking out over both Philadelphia and Camden. The water below is flat and glassy, a mirror bending every point of colored light that it catches, twisting and stretching it. Despite the lack of a breeze, he's still glad he wore a hat—woolen, and knit black; a favorite lately. He likes hiding under it, masking his horribly blond hair. Self-consciously, he tugs the hat down a little farther on his forehead. He can still feel the ends of his hair poking out the edges. Time for a haircut, he thinks... that is, if Timothy lets him. For a while now, Timothy has been the one to call the shots on everything from grooming choices to financial matters. Avery's just along for the ride.

Once, years ago, Timothy was Avery's foster brother. It didn't last long. Soon both of them were shuffled around again to new foster homes, with different foster siblings. That sense of family never left, though. The two boys were survivors, trying to find a place to belong, somewhere to thrive. In some ways, they're still looking. They both aged out of the foster care system. No longer brothers in any technical sense, now they're connected in more intimate ways, belonging only to each other rather than continuing a futile search for that elusive home ever sought in a world that doesn't seem to want them, the children left behind.

There aren't many people out tonight. He's mostly alone, and it makes him feel conspicuous. He pulls at the overlong sleeves of his slim-fitting black shirt, hiding his hands, and he ducks his head to conceal a smile as someone sprints toward him along the Ben Franklin Bridge's walkway, from the Camden side.

"Don't do it!" The teenage boy gasps, hands on knees as he catches his breath, then at his side as a muscle cramps. "Fucker. You have so much to live for! What would your mother think!?"

Avery snorts, "And who's my mother supposed to be?" He turns, leaning back instead of forward on the railing, crossing his ankles, the picture of serenity. His jeans hang low on his lean frame, and with his elbows planted on the railing, the front of his shirt pulls up in front, displaying a tantalizing strip of pale skin between his hips. "Maybe if you weren't so damn *slow*..."

"Slow?" Timothy scoffs, stepping up to Avery, straddling his legs. Usually he makes Avery feel short—at five foot eight he's two inches shorter than Timothy, but convinced he still has one more growth spurt left in him, that the relatives he never met were fantastically tall, even though he has no proof of such a thing. Leaning as he is, Timothy towers over him, so Avery glances up through the long golden bangs he hates, his big green eyes taking over his boyish face. "You had your hand down my pants, then you up and take the fuck off? How am I supposed to run after you?"

"It was pretty funny," Avery grins slyly, sliding up to his feet to use every bit of his height. The glow coming off of Philadelphia on his left makes it look like Oz, a wondrous, magical place—especially compared to darker, seedy Camden on his right. But Camden is his home now. The rent's cheap. The company is good. Letting his lips part softly, his eyes closing halfway, Avery watches Timothy's mouth. Chasing it, he stays a breath away, a smile playing at the corners of his full lips.

"Maybe," Timothy says thoughtfully, his naturally hushed, sandpapery voice like a tickle that races over Avery's skin, "I should keep you on a leash."

"Mm, kinky," Avery purrs, grabbing Timothy brazenly by the crotch. Breathing out a rush of air, Timothy shivers, squints down at him and surges for his mouth. Avery in turn leans back, keeping just out of range, thinking of the random stranger that Timothy blew the other day for a hundred bucks.

"Stop that," Timothy scolds, grabbing Avery by the back of the head, getting hat and hair both, using the grip to pull him into kissing range. The tip of Avery's tongue teases lightly over the center of Timothy's top lip and he tries to jerk away again, but Timothy yanks him close, kissing him deep and dirty until Avery's head spins. They break after long minutes. "When I want to kiss you, you have to let me."

"Oh yeah?"

"Yeah, actually. It's a rule. I just made it."

"Gonna get that tattooed on your arm too? Or maybe you could just write 'property of Timothy' over my ass."

Timothy's eyebrows shoot up. "Can I?"

Avery's response is a deep, rolling chuckle. He undulates forward, dragging in a slow grind against Timothy's groin. It makes Timothy exhale heavily, so Avery does it again but this time Timothy grabs Avery's ass to guide his movements and keep him there. Avery keeps at it until Timothy's dark brown eyes are black with lust, his skin flushed with heat. Then he wriggles away, slipping from his lover's hold and hopping a few feet down the walkway with a bright laugh.

He dashes farther away while Timothy groans and braces a hand on the railing. "How can someone so sweet be so evil?"

"It's a talent?" Avery shrugs. He makes like he's going to run away again, so Timothy fishes something from his back pocket—his wallet. Flipping it open, he holds up one of the pictures held in the plastic sleeve, waving it.

"Avery," he calls in a sing-song voice, and it's mostly that—the music of Timothy's voice, both rough and soft at the same time, that makes him stop and look.

"Oh, you son of a bitch," Avery gasps, startled, his chest suddenly tight, his knees weak. "Gimme that!" He bolts back to Timothy and lunges for the wallet, which Timothy holds away, out over the water. "Give it to me! You have that in your wallet?! You can't do that!"

"Sure I can," Timothy says easily, his smile all sweetness. "What's the matter? It's just a picture of you."

"You know what it is! Give it!"

"No way. It's my prized possession. I told you I was gonna keep it."

"Yeah, I thought you meant keep it in a private place," Avery cries, his face pink with the force of his embarrassment. It makes his lips look dark and sensual, his eyes like jewels, his hair like silk. Timothy drinks in the sight of his prize, while keeping the bait easily out of grabbing range.

"Who's going to be looking through my wallet? Huh? Nobody. It's fine."

"That was supposed to be private," Avery says a little breathlessly. His eyes shine wet, and Timothy hooks a hand around Avery's jaw, rubbing over blond stubble. Cars, trucks and motorcycles speed past, blurs of weight, noise and color, inconsequential. The only thing standing still, the only thing here is Avery, close to tears. Timothy lets him grab the wallet and holds Avery's face in two hands instead of one. He turns them, backing Avery up to an alcove, a tucked-away metal door in a tall stone column along the bridge's walkway, leading to God-knows-where, but it takes them out of the line of sight of anyone else that might be near. Hidden in shadows, surrounded by people rushing this way and that, the water sliding by under their feet and the stars spinning in the sky, Timothy kisses Avery. He kisses soft lips and sucks gently on the wicked, hot muscle of his tongue as Avery whimpers quietly and tucks the closed wallet back in Timothy's back pocket. Timothy works open the fly of Avery's pants as they both remember back to that night.

Timothy had been complaining about how he didn't have any decent photos of Avery, so Avery offered to pose for one. Timothy had taken this amazing little blue pill that helped him stay hard for a long, long time, and he made love to Avery over and over again, until he was laying boneless, sweaty, fucked-out and gorgeous on the bed. His eyes half-closed, his skin heated, his lips kiss-bitten, just basking in the afterglow. And Timothy took his picture. Just his face, from the neck up.

It was supposed to be a secret, between only them. Avery doesn't really understand why it hurt to see Timothy wave the picture around like that, but it did. A tear slides down his cheek and his fingers push up the sleeve of Timothy's right arm, tracing carefully the tender, healing skin where Timothy was tattooed a few weeks ago. Avery's fingers map the swollen letters, the A, then the V, the E. That's as far as he gets before Timothy pulls away, sinking down to his knees right there on the bridge. Using his body to protect Avery's modesty, he pulls him out and swallows him down, one hand cradling Avery's erection by the root, the other palming his bottom through his jeans.

Avery groans, letting his head fall back against the metal door. The sound is lost in the chaos of the night. The hot, wet closeness of Timothy's mouth hugs around him. It feels like coming home and then sudden intense suction makes Avery thrust helplessly. Timothy allows it, guiding him into a rhythm. Avery moans louder, the sound breaking off. Sweat beads over his skin, and the unmoving chill of the night balances the heat. Cold outside, hot within. And hot within Timothy. Avery rides him, pushing closer to orgasm. His fingers tangle in the dark-blond, tousled strands of Timothy's hair. He imagines people in the passing cars glimpsing them, there and gone, as they speed past. It gives him a thrill and edges him closer to release. He imagines a cop seeing them, too, and handcuffs, getting brought up on indecent exposure charges. Timothy fondles his balls and Avery moans thickly.

Deciding in a flash, just working on instinct alone, he digs something of his own from his back pocket. Pulling Timothy gently off of him by the hair, Avery croaks, "C'mere. Quick."

Timothy looks confused, but he stands, staying close to block Avery from view. Avery slips something into Timothy's hand. "We need to start using these. Every time. Okay?"

"Okay," Timothy nods. They lock eyes for a moment, and Avery sees the apology brewing, the heartbreak, and the hell of what Timothy has done for them, all of them. The lost and forgotten former brothers and sisters, there and gone, then back together again. That's why Avery turns away, putting his back to his lover, his best friend, his soulmate, and pushes his pants down in back just enough, giving him everything but the chance to say he's sorry.

Timothy moans, stepping up flush to him. He rolls on the pre-lubed condom Avery had passed him and gently, slowly, presses in.

Avery's mouth falls open and the night rips his cry away. For a few minutes there is only the push and pull, the thrumming of movement and racing of life through the bridge, vibrating up through their feet, the sparkle of lights, the bite of the air, the span of the sky overhead. He possesses Timothy, is full of him, aching from it; knowing he's in so deeply, Avery will never be able to get him out, not really.

A hand tugs Avery's dick and he cries out again, coming over the metal door he's pressed against. Timothy works him through it, pounding into him as he tightens up with his climax. Then he twitches, gasping roughly in Avery's ear, filling the condom, holding so tightly to Avery as everything washes away, everything but them.

The condom gets thrown in the river. Timothy zips them both up.

"I love you," Avery says quietly, unable to look at Timothy when he says it.

"I know," Timothy says, just as quietly, glancing around to make sure no police are in sight. "Come on, let's get out of here."

They slowly begin walking back toward Camden, Avery with his hands in his pockets, taking his time, still in a post-coital daze. Timothy watches him constantly out of the periphery of his vision, unable to take his eyes away from the sight of Avery's unintentional beauty. After a while, he slings an arm around Avery's shoulders, pulling him close. They walk like that to the end of the bridge.

"I'm kind of hungry," Avery murmurs, his stomach growling loudly. He's barely eaten all day — the cupboards at home have been empty for a while. No one's gone food shopping or had enough cash to do so, and eating out is too expensive. "How 'bout we swing by Sacred Heart, see if they're still serving dinner?"

Timothy's perpetually sunny face clouds over, his expression darkening. "We can pick up some dinner. I'm not taking you to the fucking soup kitchen."

"Don't worry about it, then. Never mind. I'm getting my paycheck in the morning anyway."

"Hey," Timothy comes to an abrupt halt, stopping Avery too, his arm still wound around him possessively. He closes the circle with his other arm, seeing how thin Avery is and the strain behind his eyes, far too much for an eighteen-year-old. "I'm gonna take care of us. No worries, okay?" The assurance is punctuated with a soft kiss to the furrows of concern in Avery's brow. They smooth away and Avery wraps Timothy in a hug.

"Okay. Sorry, I don't know what's wrong with me." When he pulls away, he's smiling again. "Come on. I'll race you." He fakes like he's going to take off, and at the horror that slackens Timothy's jaw, Avery bursts into wild, free laughter. "Oh my god, you should see your face!"

Rolling his eyes with relief, Timothy hooks his arm more tightly around his companion to rein him in and kisses his temple. "I don't know what your hurry is all the time anyway. You should stop and enjoy things once in a while."

Avery slings his arm around Timothy's waist, leaning on him. They disappear into the starlit night, arm in arm.

If you enjoyed this story, you can sign up for a free membership at ForbiddenFiction and discuss it with other readers and the author at the *Between Here and There* story page at http://forbiddenfiction.com/library/story/LK1-1.000014.

About the Author

Website: www.lynnkelling.com/

Lynn Kelling began writing in order to tell stories that weren't afraid of the dark, didn't hold anything back and always strived to be memorable, forging lasting attachments between character and reader. Her inspiration comes from taking a closer look at behaviors and ideas lurking at the fringes of life—basically anything that people may hesitate to speak of in mixed company, but everyone wonders about anyway. Her work is driven by the taboo in order to expose the humanity within it. Lynn is an artist, designer and lover of any form of creative self-expression that comes from a place of honesty and emotion, whether it's body art or opera. She has had multiple novels published, has written over fifty works of erotic fiction of varying lengths, and always has several novels in progress.

Works by Lynn Kelling:

Deliver Us **series:**
Deliver Us (Book 1)
From Temptation (Book 2)
Forgive Us (Book 3)

Twin Ties **series:**
My Brother's Lover (Book 1)
Twin Affairs (Book 2)

Other Works:
Whatever the Cost
Bound by Lies

Cursed Blessings (short story)

About the Publisher

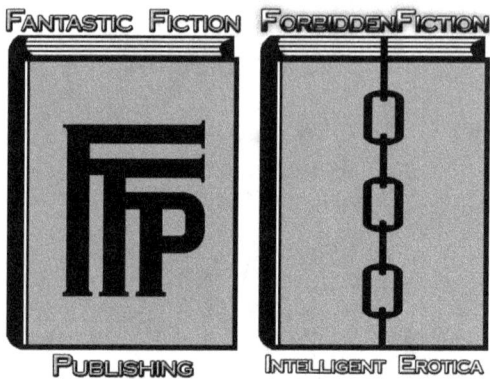

ForbiddenFiction.com is a publisher devoted to writing that breaks the boundaries of original erotic fiction. Our stories combine intense sexuality with quality writing. Stories at ForbiddenFiction.com not only arouse readers through sensations, but also engage them emotionally and mentally through storytelling as well-crafted as the sex is hot.

ForbiddenFiction.com is also designed to be a social reading environment. You'll have fun even if just reading the latest post each day, yet you will have the chance for so much more. Readers and authors can be part of ongoing discussions of specific works and individual authors as well as more general topics.

Sign up for a FREE Membership today at ForbiddenFiction.com

www.ingramcontent.com/pod-product-compliance
Lightning Source LLC
Chambersburg PA
CBHW060122260626
47160CB00005B/1979